> *"It would be best if you shared a bed with me. I will rest assured of your safety that way."*

"We agreed we'd be platonic," she said firmly. "Sex complicates things."

"So you indicated last night," he said, looking grumpy.

She laughed and then adopted a prim manner. "Putting off gratification is good for one's character, Your Highness."

"Or it may drive me to desperate acts," he retorted, and looked her over as if thinking of seizing her and making off for parts unknown.

Even if the danger he'd mentioned was real, she thought, it was worth it for these moments and the closeness she felt to this man. She suddenly wanted to say yes to his marriage proposals and to making love…and to anything else he had in mind.

LAURIE PAIGE

"One of the nicest things about writing romances is researching locales, careers and ideas. In the interest of authenticity, most writers will try anything...once." Along with her writing adventures, Laurie has been a NASA engineer, a past president of the Romance Writers of America, a mother and a grandmother. She was twice a Romance Writers of America RITA® Award finalist for Best Traditional Romance and has won awards from *Romantic Times* for Best Silhouette Special Edition and Best Silhouette in addition to appearing on the *USA TODAY* bestseller list. Recently resettled in Northern California, Laurie is looking forward to whatever experiences her next novel will send her on. After writing about Lantanya's handsome prince and new princess, soon to be king and queen, Laurie has decided she must go on a Mediterranean tour. She hopes to visit the happy royal couple....

LOGAN'S LEGACY

ROYAL AFFAIR
LAURIE PAIGE

Silhouette Books

Published by Silhouette Books
America's Publisher of Contemporary Romance

Special thanks and acknowledgment are given to Laurie Paige for her contribution to the LOGAN'S LEGACY series.

SILHOUETTE BOOKS

ISBN 0-373-61386-5

ROYAL AFFAIR

Visit Silhouette Books at www.eHarlequin.com

Printed in U.S.A.

Be a part of

$\mathscr{L}$OGAN'S $\mathscr{L}$EGACY

*Because birthright has its privileges
and family ties run deep.*

Their passionate encounter had more than
one consequence…!

Prince Maxwell von Husden: He needed to
find a bride—and quickly. He'd seduced beautiful
Ivy Crosby and now she carried his baby—the
future king of Lantanya. His country needed
leadership, and he needed Ivy. Could he convince
her to walk down the aisle?

Ivy Crosby: A night of passion with a mysterious
man landed Ivy Crosby in the tabloids. When she
met Max, she had no idea he was royalty. And
now this prince was offering her the chance to be
his princess! But she'd have to teach him a thing or
two about love—and romance—first!

Everett Baker: He had a wicked crush on
Nurse Nancy, but was there another reason
he was courting the warm and trusting R.N.?

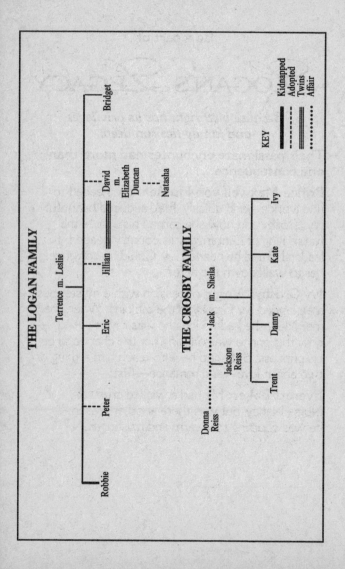

THE LOGAN FAMILY

Terrence m. Leslie

Robbie   Peter   Eric   Jillian   David
m.
Elizabeth
Duncan

Bridget

Natasha

THE CROSBY FAMILY

Jack   m. Sheila

Donna
Reiss

Jackson
Reiss

Trent   Danny   Kate   Ivy

KEY

Kidnapped
Adopted
Twins
Affair

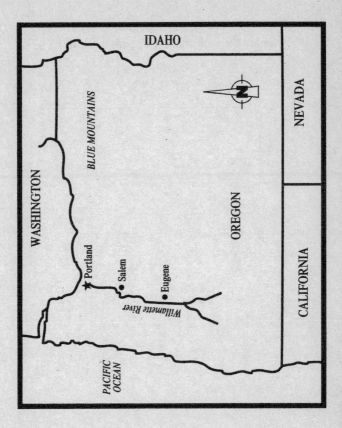

For Di and friends—
we are the stuff that dreams are made of.

One

Ivy Crosby stood in the checkout line at the drug-store and wished someone would remove the display of gilt-framed mirrors, marked down fifty percent for quick sale, from the wall to her right. The mirrors reflected multiple images and she really didn't want to see herself just now.

With a grimace she reached up to tuck a strand of hair behind her ear. It didn't stay, of course.

Her hair was naturally blond, not always an asset, and naturally curly, which meant it did as it pleased. On an impulse she couldn't explain, she'd had the long tresses cut off last week.

A mistake, that. Now it lay in ringlets around her face, making her look about seven instead of twenty-seven. She was also cursed with big blue eyes and a natural fringe of dark lashes that curled at the tips just like her hair.

The combination lent her a fragile innocence that was sometimes useful in business, but was mostly irritating as people took her at face value.

Because of her looks, she'd been treated like a pet or a doll all her life. By family. By teachers. By boyfriends who'd been protective and possessive, as if they wanted to put her in a pocket and only let her out when it was convenient. For them.

Except for one man. Once upon a fairy tale time out of time, she'd met her prince—a man who'd treated her as a woman, a very desirable woman, an equal in wit, intelligence...and passion.

Oh, yes, passion. A faint tremor ran through her blood, the first warning of the volcanic explosion that was to come. Just the thought of him, six weeks later, could do that to her.

Max. I need you.

No, she mentally chided. She was an adult and she could figure this out. But first things first, as one of her business professors used to say. That was why she was at this pharmacy in a strip mall where she wasn't likely to be recognized.

Her many images glowered at her from the mirrors. She smoothed out the frown and laid her purchases on the counter. She'd gotten lotion and shampoo and a couple of other things she didn't need in hopes that no one would notice she'd also gotten a pregnancy test kit.

"Sorry, I have to change the tape," the clerk said, opening the top of the cash register and removing the spent roll of paper. When she attempted to thread the new roll through the machine, it jammed. The woman muttered a curse.

Ivy tamped down the impatience that made her want to turn and walk out as fast as she could. She'd stood in line this long, what was a few more minutes? Besides, she would have to do it all over again someplace else.

Schooling herself to calmness, she absently glanced over the tabloids while she waited. The headlines were amusing as usual—Woman Gives Birth to Martian and other interesting tidbits.

She skimmed the large print. A movie star was getting a divorce. Ho-hum. The Lion Roars, proclaimed another above a picture of a handsome man holding the arm of a fragile beauty—

Ivy gasped. She grabbed the edge of the counter as the room went into a dangerous spin.

"Are you all right?" the clerk asked, leaning close and peering into her eyes.

Ivy blinked several times and the world righted itself. Except for the abyss giving way under her feet. "Yes, just a…a sort of…of a dizzy spell. I'm fine now." She smiled to prove that she was.

The clerk nodded sympathetically. "When I was pregnant with my first, I fainted at the drop of a hat. Blood was especially bad. My sister cut her finger one night when we were having dinner at her place. I fell right out on the kitchen floor. Scared my husband to death. He didn't know I was expecting. Neither did I, come to think of it."

Ivy dredged up a smile while the clerk and the woman behind her in line laughed nostalgically. "I'll take this, too," she said, and put the tabloid on the counter.

By the time she'd paid cash for her purchases and rushed to her car, every nerve in her body was quivering like an aspen leaf in a playful breeze. As she got in, she tossed her purchases into the passenger seat, grabbed the tabloid and read the article that went with the headline.

Her eyes widened and narrowed by turns as she skimmed through the hyperbole to get to the meat of the story. It seemed Prince Maxwell von Husden, Crown Prince of Lantanya, who was soon to be king, had been seen at a popular tourist resort in the tiny country with a mysterious beauty in July. After a romantic night of dining and dancing and passion, the woman had disappeared.

Ivy gasped and felt faint again. How could they have known about the passion?

Reporters always made up the stuff to fill in the blanks, she decided grimly, trying to calm the emotions that roared through her like a tsunami. She read on.

The prince was furious that the woman had slipped out on him before he grew bored and dropped her, according to one "close palace source." Another source contended that the prince was heartbroken but covering it with anger.

Ivy pressed a hand to her thundering heart. "Liar," she said. She'd been right to leave without waking him the next morning, although it had been difficult to do.

He'd looked so handsome lying in the king-size bed, his hair mussed and a morning beard shadowing his face, his expression one of contentment. She'd contemplated kissing him goodbye, but she'd had a plane to catch and she wasn't sure they could stop at one kiss.

Again passion flared at the memory. She clenched the steering wheel and closed her eyes, slowly winning control of the hunger running through her.

"Are you sure you're all right?" a voice asked through the window.

She opened her eyes with a jerk and stared at the woman who'd been in line behind her. "Oh. Oh, yes. Thank you." She smiled brightly, her heart pounding so hard she could hear each beat in her ears.

The woman, who looked fortyish and had a certain world-weariness in her eyes, smiled, too. "Take care of yourself," she advised in a kindly tone and walked to a car in the next row.

Ivy composed herself and drove out of the parking lot to an apartment complex recently built on the outskirts of the city. Portland General Hospital was the next exit off the highway. At least she was close to medical care in case her heart gave out completely.

The cynical thought evaporated after she got inside her place, the door closed and locked as if a whole platoon of reporters might come charging after her.

She read the article again, then looked through the whole tabloid in case there was more information.

There wasn't. All the reporter really knew was that she and Max had had a late supper at the resort. And that the prince seemed to have been in a bad mood of late.

For a while she sat there in a stupor, shocked that the handsome, humorous, beguiling man she'd met wasn't Max Hughes, a foreigner attending to business matters in Lantanya the same as she was. She stared at the grainy print as if that could change the images in the photo that was snapped without her knowledge six weeks and four days ago.

However, the woman, whose face was partially turned from the camera, was her, and the man, who was smiling right into the lens, was apparently the man who was due to be crowned Maxwell V, King of Lantanya, in a few weeks.

The tiny island country was nestled in the Adriatic Sea, a perfect Brigadoon hidden from the rest of the world and far from reality.

Way far from reality, she silently admitted, feeling beyond foolish. Her family was right to treat her like a baby. She needed a keeper.

Laying the paper on the coffee table and leaning her head on the sofa back, she closed her eyes and groaned. A playboy prince. She'd fallen right into the lying, deceitful arms of a playboy prince. A last fling before he assumed the duties of king?

Get real. Did leopards change their spots? He would simply move on to being a playboy king. And she'd fallen for his charm, his wit, his warmth…the timbre of his deep voice, the passion in his eyes, the odd glimpses of sadness in his expression…. She'd thought they were soul mates.

A lie. It had all been a lie. And she'd believed it. Every word. He must have thought it amusing—the naive American…the shy virgin….

"Ohhh," she moaned and buried her face in her hands.

How could she have allowed herself to be taken in like that? She was smart. She'd graduated with honors in systems management and computer science. With her team of workers, she'd devised a brilliant network for the kingdom's education program—

Oh, no! She would have to go back. She might even have to face him.

The plastic bag containing her purchases rattled against her leg as she shifted in despair. Slowly she removed a small square box and stared at it as if viewing a poison potion she was supposed to drink.

"The moment of truth," she said to it.

This was indeed such a moment. It was time to confirm her direst suspicions and find out if her magical night of passion had left her with a little souvenir of the evening.

She dropped the satiric mood at the thought of a child, a sweet innocent who'd had no say in its conception, and laid a hand protectively over her abdomen.

Her home life hadn't been great during her growing years. She'd wanted better for her children. A loving family. A faithful mate. Honor and integrity and caring. She had screwed up royally.

"Ha-ha," she muttered at the unintended pun.

Rising, she walked down the short hallway to the master bedroom. Its furnishings didn't comfort her as they usually did. She'd picked them out upon leaving the family mansion and moving to the apartment in a bid for independence shortly after agreeing to work at the family business.

Well, she'd needed a job. The dot-com where she'd started right out of college had made it four years before crashing. She'd learned a lot about computer systems during that time, so she was a valuable employee.

Not that anyone else thought so. Her fellow analysts thought she was a pretty face who'd gotten her position due to family connections. That much was true, in that her sister had pressured her to come into the company.

Ivy had gladly taken on the job of bringing Lantanya's educational facilities into the twenty-first century when no one else had wanted the time-consuming task, which had included long flights across the Atlantic to Rome. She'd then had to take a puddle jumper, as some called the small jet, to Lantanya, which lay off the eastern coast of Italy in the Adriatic Sea, which was really an arm of the Mediterranean.

On the latest trip, she'd stayed in the tiny country for two months, then on her last night she'd met Max. Her own Prince Charming.

The royal liar, she dubbed him, seizing anger as a means to control the hurt she didn't want to recognize.

Going into the bathroom, she closed the door and locked it behind her. Which was ridiculous since there was no one in the apartment but her.

Really, it was a tad late to be locking herself into bathrooms to ensure that she was alone. She should have done that six weeks and four days ago, in the middle of July when she was in Lantanya instead of the first Tuesday in September, back at her apartment in Portland, Oregon.

In reality, she should have returned home before she gave in to the madness that had danced through her like bubbles from the finest champagne. She frowned and opened the pregnancy kit.

A few minutes later she emerged, shaken and chastened. She studied the results again. There was no mistake. She was expecting a child, a royal baby…and heir to the House of von Husden.

Well, probably not. Illegitimate children didn't inherit anything. She sighed shakily. As long as she kept the father a secret people might wonder about the sire, but her child wouldn't be made to feel he or she had been rejected. She would see to that. She would love her child so much, he or she would never notice the lack of a father's care.

Going out on the balcony, intending to think the situation through and come to a decision, she stared at the hills and thought of another place and another time….

"What do you think?" an amused male voice had asked.

Ivy had turned from the painting she'd been

studying to the source of the question. A tall man, probably six feet or so, a good seven or eight inches taller than she was at any rate, stood a couple of feet behind her.

He had black hair and deep-brown eyes. His skin was tanned, making his smile brilliant. His face was lean, all hard planes and angles, but put together so the whole was very handsome. There was a hint of silver at his temples, lending a distinguished air to his appearance. In spite of that, she judged his age to be in the midthirties at most.

"I'm not sure what to think," she admitted, turning back to the painting so she wouldn't stare at the alluring stranger. "I'm sure the artist has a point, but I don't think I get it."

"Same here," her fellow museum visitor agreed. "I like faces in the ordinary arrangement. Which can sometimes be quite lovely."

He gazed at her appreciatively.

A slight disappointment rose in her. Just another Lothario, she deduced. "Yes," she said coolly, as if speaking of the picture, and walked on to the next gilt-framed oil.

"I've offended you. I'm sorry. You are quite lovely, you know, but I'll try to refrain from mentioning it again."

His candor surprised her, causing her to meet his eyes. His smile was so engaging, she had to return it.

"There's a wing on this side that I think you might enjoy more," he said, gesturing to a wide, elaborately framed wooden archway and bowing in a brief but stately manner. He didn't try to guide her or touch her in any way.

"Ah," she murmured at the doorway.

A huge painting of flowers, done in the loveliest hues imaginable, was the focal point at the end of the gallery.

"It's like stepping into a garden, isn't it?" he said softly. "You can almost feel the warmth of the sunshine striking the treetops, then the coolness of the shade as you walk into the shadow of the leaf canopy."

The oddest thing was that she could. She looked at him in amazement. His smile…oh, his smile. It knew everything she was thinking….

Returning to the present, Ivy stared at the colors of the sunset lightly grazing the maple trees on the lawn and the alders closer to the creek that separated the residential complex from the golf course. The creek flowed into the Columbia River that had awed Lewis and Clark on their expedition. A much smaller river ran from the Lantanya mountains where the resort was perched down to the wine-colored sea where St. Ansellmo, the capital city of the island kingdom, lay against the shore.

She and the man who introduced himself as Max Hughes had wandered through the rest of the museum and taken tea in the garden there. They'd had the place to themselves. It had seemed as if they were the only people in the world as they talked. He'd admitted he liked to sketch the odd scene now and then, even to paint if he had time.

"Like Churchill," she'd said, "something to relax you."

"What do you do in your spare time?" he'd asked.

"Read. Go on long walks. Work on computer programs."

That was when he'd questioned her about her work. She'd told him about Crosby Systems and her job in Lantanya. He'd been keenly interested and had asked a thousand questions. When she'd asked, he said he was in business, too, mostly as a consultant. His manner had been sardonic as he admitted that last one.

Consultant? Yes, if one stretched the definition of king. Maybe he was more of a figurehead than a ruler, though.

Not that it mattered to her. He'd walked her partway back to the resort, then had to leave for a meeting. She'd been disappointed as she wound her way up the steep slope to the castle-like building on a rocky promontory.

"I'll see you again," he'd promised, briefly lifting her hand to his lips.

And he had.

Hearing music from a car passing on the street, Ivy was thrust back into the recent past and that magic night....

A cool breeze blew off the sea and music that filled her soul wafted over her as she'd stood on the patio and observed the very last of the colors in the sunset sink into the sea. She'd been alone.

"Let's not waste the music," an amused voice said from the shadows.

A man, tall, with dark hair and eyes and a brilliant smile, stepped into view. Max held his hands out and she stepped into them as if they'd done this a thousand times before. The music rose and throbbed and they dipped and swayed to the notes, wrapped in the magic of it all.

When it stopped, they did, too. They dropped their arms, but didn't move away.

"That was enchanting," he murmured, his gaze warm and filled with laughter as he studied her.

"I feel like an enchanted princess," she said, then looked at him quickly to see if she'd been too bold.

"And I, your devoted knight," he murmured, a devilish light in his eyes. He executed a smart little bow.

On impulse she nodded regally, her mouth curling with laughter at their acting. And the fact that he'd returned.

"Your meeting, did it go well?" she asked.

He shrugged. "It is concluded." His smile flashed again. "Please, Your Highness," he begged, "give me some daring feat to perform so that I may show my devotion and my sorrow that I had to leave you this afternoon."

She looked around the darkened patio, at the sky, then the capital city lying on the coast, its lights glittering like jewels. On a nearby trellis, she saw what she wanted.

"Sir Knight, there is one thing, a rose, the most perfect bloom of them all, that I crave, but it is out of my reach."

"Show it to me and it shall be yours." He dropped

to his knee. "Or by my honor and my good name, I shall perish in the attempt."

"Nay," she whispered, held by the strong, sensuous line of his lips. "You shall not perish. I won't allow it."

"Then tell me where it is."

"There." She turned from him and the allure of his smile, of his eyes and the fires that now burned hotly in those dark depths. Pointing to the highest branch and the farthest rose that wafted beyond the stone of the patio's walls, she waited breathlessly to see what he would do.

"An easy task," he told her.

He leaped to a chair, a table, then the top of the wall. Without testing the support of the trellis, he stepped upon it and climbed upward, careful of the thorny vines. When he was as high as he could go, he leaned out…and out…and out…

For a moment it seemed to her that he hung between earth and air, attached to neither, as the land dropped sharply off the bluff where the resort was built. Then he deftly plucked the rose she'd indicated, leaped back to the wall, then onto the patio and, again kneeling on one foot, presented the prize to her.

When she hesitated, feeling it was too intimate a gift, he stood and moved close. "You cannot refuse," he said in a low, husky voice, "when I have risked all for it. And for you."

He removed the thorns from the stem and tucked the pure white rose into the bosom of her blouse.

"That is where it belongs, next to your heart," he said in the same tone that sent sprinkles of stardust swirling down to the innermost parts of her.

The music began again, and they danced without speaking for a long time. From the town a clock struck the hour, a plangent vibration that echoed in her heart with each peal.

"Midnight," she whispered.

"Must you leave?"

She shook her head and looked at her feet, half expecting to find glass slippers. He followed her gaze.

His chuckle made her laugh, too. "We are foolish together, but it is fun, yes?"

She nodded. They danced some more, then went inside for a late supper. Over the meal, they talked about everything. Their lives. Their early dreams. Then later ones. Their sorrows. His mother had died two years ago, his father last fall. Max had traveled the world since then, but there had been no escaping the mourning. He had loved them very much.

"I'm so sorry," she said, taking his hand and pressing it to her cheek. "My parents are divorced, but at least I still have them both. And a stepmother."

"She doesn't like you?" His eyes became dangerous.

"Oh, yes. She's very nice."

"But?" When she looked at him perplexed, he added, "There's always more after such faint praise."

"Well, she's always been closer to my sister, Katie. Katie's a year older than I am and my best friend. I'm the baby of the family. They treat me like a pet."

He laughed at that and playfully patted her head. She snarled and pretended to bite his hand. Then they fell silent and simply observed each other over the flicker of the candle.

"I have a suite," he finally said. "I will make for you the most delicious dessert. Will you come with me and let me serve you, sweet princess of the rose?"

She nodded.

He stood and took her hand, helping her from the chair, then they drifted up the marble stairs and along a silent corridor until they came to two magnificent doors carved with two lions raised on their hind legs, their forepaws touching as they gazed fiercely at the onlooker.

"Lions rampant," he said, seeing her interest. "From the royal crest."

"A crest, like a family crest, dukes and all that?"

"Or a king, yes. The lions depict a battle between two brothers of the same house. After nearly killing each other, they decided to join forces and save the kingdom from outsiders, hence the two lions."

"Is that what happened in Lantanya?" she asked.

He nodded, then swung open one of the doors, disclosing an opulent room of crystal chandeliers, polished black granite and mirrors softly reflecting the view from every wall. She was speechless. Not even her father's house was this grand.

"This is magnificent. Who are you?" she asked, knowing she must look like a wide-eyed naif.

"Just a man," he said, turning her toward him and holding her lightly, carefully in his arms. "One who has been enchanted by moonlight and music…and one very special rose."

She shivered at the intensity in his voice and looked away as the innate shyness possessed her.

"You are a shy princess," he murmured.

"Yes. Katie and I are the quiet ones," she explained, referring to her sibling. "We have two brothers, both older. Trent is CEO of the company. Danny…well, he's been living in seclusion since too many tragedies took their toll on him."

"I see." He took her hand. "Now about that dessert." Ivy was glad he picked up on the fact that discussing Danny was too personal.

In a kitchen that had more marble and polished granite than a museum, he prepared cherries jubilee. After flipping out the lights and setting the cherries aflame, he spooned the concoction over ice cream and set a large bowl in front of her.

"I can't possibly eat this much," she protested.

He handed her a silver spoon with the lion crest and took one for himself. "Not alone perhaps. I shall help."

With her sitting on one side of a marble counter and him standing on the other, they ate spoonfuls of the dessert when the flames died and gazed at each other, their eyes saying more than the few words they shared. Soon the treat was gone.

When she started to pat her mouth one last time with the linen napkin, he caught her hand, then kissed her with the greatest tenderness she'd ever known.

Underscoring the tenderness was the passion.

She sensed it in him as a great force, a river that ran silently and deep, a part of his being, and she knew instinctively that it was more than desire, although that was there, too.

She gave herself to the kiss and to the passion and the desire…and to him….

Two

Maxwell von Husden, Prince Regent of Lantanya, was having a bad day. He'd had a bad week... month...in fact, the whole year had been rotten.

His restless gaze stopped on a vase of roses, white with a coral blush, fresh from the royal gardens.

Except for one night of splendor, he amended his earlier observation. That one night with *the rose,* as he thought of her to himself in the few moments of privacy he had before falling into an exhausted sleep, had been the one grace note of the summer, a gift he'd never expected. The gods had been kind—

A discreet knock on the door preceded the entrance of his valet. "Ready, Your Highness?" Ned Bartlett asked, looking him over like a mother with a youngster heading for his first day of school.

The man's ancestors had served the kings of Lantanya, the third longest continuous monarchy in Europe after Britain and the Netherlands, almost as long as the kingdom had existed. And they were as thoroughly English as the British crown.

"Yes."

Their eyes met in the mirror. Max recognized sympathy in the valet's familiar gray eyes. Fifteen years older than his own thirty-three years, Bartlett was the only person alive who had witnessed the tears and sorrows of a young prince growing to manhood under the watchful eyes of his parents and the residents of the kingdom. The valet had been his most constant companion from the time he was six.

Taking a deep breath, Max let it out and with it the doubts and pain of what was to come. Today he would pass a life sentence on his uncle, his dead father's half brother, and on the former minister of state, for high treason.

During the traditional year of mourning after his father's death, the two men had planned a coup to take over the country before Max was formally crowned at the end of the grieving period. With the deed accomplished, they would then deny him reentry into the country.

Max had unexpectedly returned from eight restless, sorrow-driven months abroad a day before the attempt. That night, hired assassins had broken into his bedroom, planning to kill him.

Only he wasn't there. He'd been at the resort, sleeping peacefully—his last night of rest in over six weeks—in the arms of the rose. The need to be with her had been stronger than the prickles of his conscience, urging him to return to the palace.

Staying with her had saved his life.

As for the traitors, confusion at not finding the prince in his bed had destroyed the attackers' plans and timing. The royal palace guards had seen the men and arrested them.

The next morning, upon his return, he and the guards, assisted by his security advisor, had arrested the main culprits, his uncle and the minister, and quelled the coup before it had a chance to get started, much less succeed.

During the past month, the culprits had been tried by the High Court, composed of the twelve lord mayors, each representing one of the twelve counties of the country. The three members of the Supreme Court had sat as judges over the proceedings.

Today was the last step—the formal sentencing. Only the king could do that since it was a case of high treason. His title was Prince Regent until the coronation ceremony, but he was the ruler and the job was his.

"Will I do?" he asked impatiently.

After Bartlett had pronounced him fit to be seen, he left his suite in the residential side of the palace and strode toward the justice chamber where much of the business of the kingdom was conducted. He glanced at a portrait of a sixteenth-century ancestor as he strode the long corridor separating the two areas.

That particular king had been beheaded by a trusted friend while they were having dinner in the king's apartment. Again loyal officers had saved the day and the infant prince and, therefore, the kingdom.

"There, but for the grace of God and an ironic twist of fate, I almost went," he murmured, his blood warming at the memory of that night and the woman who had been as stirred as he by their kisses.

A door opened to his left, and his security advisor, who'd been his roommate and best friend at university in the U.S., stepped out. Like Bartlett, Chuck Curland looked him over as if to detect any cracks in his armor.

"I'm all right," Max said tersely, although he hadn't been asked.

His friend opened a door with a digital security lock, something new in the palace. All outside doors had already been converted. Inside ones were next, particularly his quarters. Dead bolts and high-tech locks. In a palace that hadn't been locked since being built two hundred years ago.

Max entered the armory and strapped on the golden jewel-encrusted sheath and sword of the head of state. He left off the sash with its brooches and badges of honor. This was not a ceremonial occasion, only a punishing one. The sword of justice represented that fact.

"Do I look regal enough?" he asked, his smile tinged with bitterness at the thought of what was ahead.

"Royal to the bone," Chuck assured him, grasping his shoulder briefly.

Few men would have dared touch him, but Max knew the gesture from his friend was one of solidarity. He turned and walked into the Justice Chamber before he blubbered like a baby at the betrayal of his uncle and the minister he'd also trusted. Kings were not allowed emotion.

"All rise," the sergeant-at-arms intoned.

The court and its audience rose as one, heads bowed, as he took his place on the high seat behind the three justices. When he was seated, the crowd sat, too.

The bailiff presented the case to the king.

"Has the jury reached a verdict?" Max asked. As if he didn't know.

"We have, Your Majesty," the lord high mayor said.

The sergeant-at-arms received the signed verdict from the mayor and delivered it to the senior judge of the Supreme Court, who silently read it, let his two cohorts see it, then presented it to the prince regent.

Max read the paper, then, setting his face to no expression, spoke, "Lord High Mayor, how find the jury on the first charge?"

"We, the jury, find the defendants guilty," the man said.

"Lord High Mayor, how find the jury on the second charge?" Max continued the formalized ritual.

"Guilty."

The third charge?

"Guilty."

The fourth?

"Guilty," the head of the jury replied.

Max experienced not satisfaction but a great sorrow as the men were found guilty on all counts—treason, attempt to murder a head of state, conspiracy to overthrow the rightful succession of the kingdom, use of violence against a member of the royal house.

Gloom settled in his spirit like great weights strapped to his soul. Through the high, stained-glass windows of the courtroom, the world seemed to darken.

Ah, rose, I need you.

"Is the court ready for the sentencing?" he asked.

"The court is ready," the senior supreme justice told him. "The defendants will rise," he instructed.

Max sentenced his uncle and the minister to ninety-nine years in prison. Even after their deaths, their remains would stay in the prison cemetery until the full ninety-nine years were up before relatives could claim the bodies.

The two captains of the Royal Dragoons who had joined them in the conspiracy were given life sentences with no chance of parole.

The two hired assassins, who were not citizens of Lantanya, had already been tried in a lower court and sentenced to life. The men would work at hard labor and have no chance of getting out for thirty years.

At the end of two hours it was finished.

When Max returned to his quarters, his dress uniform was damp under the arms and down his back from the tension of sentencing four men he'd known from birth to a prison routine filled with work and, when not working, isolation.

Their lives would be almost as lonely as that of a king.

Bartlett quietly entered and removed the used clothing. "Will you be needing anything further?" he asked in the gentle tones he'd always used when Max had been a child and suffered some bereavement to his young soul.

"No, thanks. I'll take a shower, then ring for Chuck when I'm dressed. Perhaps coffee when he arrives?"

"Muffins and fruit would be nice, too," the valet suggested. "You haven't eaten."

Max nodded. "Okay. Give me twenty minutes. And, Ned, thank you." He wasn't sure what he was thanking him for. Perhaps for his unspoken sympathy, or his eternal kindness, or for simply being here when things got tough.

The older man nodded solemnly. "My pleasure, sir."

Alone, Max quickly showered and dried, then returned to the bedroom to dress. Stopping by the reading table, he lifted one perfect rose from the bouquet and sniffed the delicate perfume.

He closed his eyes as memory poured through him. In an uncharacteristic gesture, he brought the flower to his lips, feeling the fragile coolness of its petals. A shudder went through him as the vast emptiness of his chambers assailed his heart. For that one night he hadn't been alone....

"You're trembling," he had said, drawing back a little from the kiss, reluctant to let go of the treasure of her mouth.

"It's…I don't know what it is," she'd admitted. "It's all so strange. The night…the whole day… seems like a dream. Unreal." She laid her hands against his chest. "And yet so real."

"I know." He gazed deeply into her eyes, their blue depths so clear it was like looking into her innermost thoughts. He saw doubt and uncertainty, but also passion and intrigue. All the things that raged through him in undulating waves of desire. "I've never felt this way before, not about anyone."

"Nor have I," she said, gazing at him with a worried frown on her beautiful face.

He kissed her cheek, along her jaw, then behind her ear, careful of the tiny gold earrings she wore. Against his chest, he felt her breasts rise with a quickly drawn breath. A groan of need escaped him as the passion rose higher between them. Her arms crept around his neck as he drew her tight against him, unable to disguise the strength of his response to her.

For a time he was content to hold and kiss her, to stroke her back, her arms, her sides. Then that wasn't enough. He'd always made it a point never to become involved with anyone not of his set, women who knew the rules and expected only a night of pleasure with no promises.

He wanted to make promises to this woman, he found. Words like *forever* danced on the tip of his tongue. He closed his eyes and tried to clear his mind.

When she swayed against him in sweet surrender, rational thinking scattered like birds before a storm. He cupped her hips in both hands and rubbed against her, needing full body contact.

"Beautiful princess, will you stay?" he asked, oddly humbled by the passion in her eyes and the sweet confusion in her trembling lips. "Say yes," he urged, afraid she was going to say no.

"I…I may not please you," she whispered.

A realization came to him. "Are you an untried rose, opening her petals for the first time?"

White teeth sank into beguiling pink lips, kissed bare of makeup long ago. He hardly heard her answer.

"Yes," she finally said, pressing her face against his throat in sweet embarrassment.

A tenderness, so strong it was almost an ache, spread through him. "I'll be gentle," he promised, "if you're willing. If this is what you want."

An eternity passed between one heartbeat and another, then she lifted her head, met his eyes and nodded. She was brave, and she was his. *His.*

Golden stardust seemed to shower them in magic. They were surrounded by it, then suffused with it as they kissed again. He touched her hair, her face, then her breasts, feeling the hard points of passion there at the tips.

Without releasing her lips, he lifted her, then carried her to the bedroom. Although she was shy, there was no awkwardness between them as he undressed her, then himself.

Once nude, he clasped her slender body to his, letting the full tactile sensation of skin against skin flow over them as they touched, chest, belly, thighs. When he stripped back the covers, they fell onto the sheets as one, laughter bubbling between them in that mysterious sharing of feelings that had happened nearly from the first moment they met.

When he pressed lightly on her shoulder, she lay back and let him gaze his fill at her.

"Breathtaking," he murmured.

"So are you," she said with a little catch as her gaze ran over him.

He wondered if he frightened her with his blatant male desire that couldn't be hidden as easily as hers could. With the gentlest touch, he stroked from her shoulder, over her breast, down her abdomen and to her thigh. Then he paid homage to her breasts with his hands and his mouth.

When he probed her belly button with his tongue, it made her laugh. He smiled at her, then went back to the exploration that tantalized them both to near madness. When he kissed along her thighs, first one, then the other, she gasped.

Her eyes grew big when he glanced up, then nudged her legs apart, asking entry to the secret treasure that was hers to give or withhold.

"Please," he murmured, "I need to taste you."

When he'd brought her to the peak once, then twice, he finally heeded her little cries that he come to her.

"At once," she said. "Now. I want you. I want everything."

The red heat of desire shimmered between them. He observed the flush that caused her skin to glow as it swept up her chest and into her cheeks, telling him of her growing hunger and feeding his own until his mind was hazy with it.

"I've never wanted a woman this way," he whispered. "This much."

"How much?" she asked with such innocence it seared his heart.

"With everything in me. As if the world would perish in one of your tender sighs if we didn't share this. As if my life depended on this one moment. On you—"

Max crushed the rose in his fist, jolted out of the lovely remembrance by the knowledge that his life *had* depended on her at that exact moment. Their passion had literally saved him from the assassins. Would he ever get a chance to tell her?

"I must leave tomorrow," she'd said when they had consummated the union and lay entwined in blissful contentment after he'd taken care of her with a warm washcloth and a towel tucked under her hips.

He smiled now, recalling the blushes and her embarrassed protests, which he'd ignored.

"No," he'd said, the command of a king if she'd but known it.

"I have to. I have a job to do." She'd sighed plaintively.

He'd tightened his arms around her. "I will follow you to the ends of the earth," he'd vowed.

Releasing the crushed rose, he dropped it into the

wastebasket. The conspiracy had taken all his time and attention during the next six weeks. His presence as king, in deed if not yet in name, had been required. Now that the trial and sentencing were finished, he could think of other things, like finding his rose.

Quickly dressing in jeans and a T-shirt, he grabbed the phone and punched in his security advisor's private number.

Chuck answered on the first ring.

"Can you come to my quarters?" Max asked.

"Be right there."

No sooner had he hung up, than a knock sounded on his door. "Come in."

Bartlett entered with a serving cart. On it were a coffee urn, two cups, two plates and a platter of muffins, plus another with a variety of fruit. He didn't know how the man knew exactly when to arrive, but it had been this way since Max's earliest memories in the palace.

"Thanks, Bartlett. I'll be going out for a hike in about an hour."

"Very good, sir." The man left as quietly as he'd entered, leaving the door ajar and speaking to someone in the hall.

Chuck Curland came inside and closed the door, then pulled the pocket doors from their hiding place and closed them, too. Two sets of doors had been built into all the king's rooms when the palace was constructed to ensure privacy in conversation. Max, upon his father's advice, used them.

"Coffee?" Max asked.

"Please." The American glanced around the room the way he did each time he entered.

Once, Max had teased him about expecting a spy behind every curtain. Lately the idea didn't seem funny.

Chuck's eyes were light blue and seemed to see everything that might be the slightest suspicious. His hair was brown with blond streaks from their hours of jogging on the beach. His frame matched Max's inch for inch, pound for pound. In college they'd shared a room the first semester, then, finding they got along superbly, an apartment after that until they graduated.

Chuck was five years older than Max and had been an Army Ranger before going to school on the G.I. bill. That the two had met at all was a demonstration of American democracy in action when they'd been randomly assigned to share a room.

Max's father, the late king, had suggested Chuck come to Lantanya and advise them on security matters. Perhaps the king had known at that early stage of their friendship that Max would need a friend in the palace. Chuck, with his all-seeing gaze, had detected the conspiracy and warned Max, thus bringing him home early.

Max poured the coffee and filled a plate, then sat in his favorite chair. Chuck did the same.

"This reminds me of days with my father," Max told his friend. "Except, the king sat where I am, in a big black leather chair, and I sat in this chair, which was located where you are."

"What happened to the king's chair?" Chuck asked, taking a muffin and several spoons of fruit.

"I had it placed in the royal museum along with his suit of armor and ceremonial outfits."

Chuck smiled. "Are you going to have armor made for yourself?"

"No. The bulletproof vest you insisted I buy is more than enough for my tastes."

"It's more effective when it's worn," Chuck said dryly.

Max cocked one eyebrow. "I'm not going to sleep in it, and that's final."

They smiled at each other with the ease of companions who'd seen each other puking their guts out after their first—and last—overindulgence in beer, moaning over the fickleness of college girls who threw them over for the captain of the football team and cursing their professors for tests that were impossible to pass.

"Speaking of sleeping. Or not sleeping, as the case may be..." Chuck said, the words trailing off as he studied Max with his omniscient gaze.

Max tossed him a questioning glance as he bit into a muffin. It seemed odd, in light of the morning activities, to realize he was hungry. Life had a way of going on, he reasoned.

Chuck lifted a muffin. "You gotta get married," he said, and took a bite.

Max nearly choked. "What the hell brought that on?"

His friend chewed and swallowed, then took a sip of coffee. "Last year, before he died, your father made me promise to see that you found a bride by the end of the mourning period. You must produce an heir."

Max muttered a curse, then another. Neither helped calm the swirl of emotion in his breast.

Chuck observed him with an odd little smile playing about the corners of his mouth. "An heiress will do," he continued. "Either English or European would be acceptable to your people. Or American."

Max glared when a full smile broke over his friend's face. There was knowledge in those blue eyes that said Chuck knew more than he was saying.

"Spit it out," he invited, knowing there was more.

"Your tryst at the resort probably saved your life, or at least prevented a nasty injury. I like to tell myself that the guards, whom I trained, would have interceded before great bodily harm was done."

"Yeah. Me, too."

"So?"

"So?" Max echoed, not sure what the question was.

"Is it the American?"

Like the petals of a flower suddenly clamping shut, Max withdrew, not wanting to share that night with anyone, not even his best friend. He shook his head slightly, not in denial of the possibility, but of sharing it.

"She might be pregnant," Chuck said and calmly put the rest of the muffin in his mouth.

Max sprang to his feet as if an electric current had suddenly run through his chair. He paced to the window. The vase of roses blew gentle kisses of sweet scent at him. He paused and touched one.

"What makes you think that?" he finally asked.

"I'm your security chief, Your Highness. I'm paid to know what goes on around you."

Chuck always reverted to formalities when he gained insights into Max's life that might transgress friendship. Max appreciated the gesture. That left it up to him to decide the level of the discussion.

"She was a virgin," Max said softly.

"Yes, sir."

"It was a night like none other," he continued. "When I ran out of condoms, I took a chance with her. How did you know that?"

"There was, uh, evidence on the sheets. I took the liberty of confiscating them…in case there were future questions about the child's conception, if there should happen to be a child."

"In case I got whacked," Max said sardonically, catching on to his advisor's line of reasoning.

However, his demise wasn't uppermost in his mind at the moment. He recalled pulling the petals from a dozen roses and sprinkling them over the bed and her. His friend would have seen those, too, and known what a sentimental fool Max had made of himself. He groaned internally.

Chuck studied him for a long minute, then smiled in understanding. "Are you in love with the American beauty?" he asked, one friend to another.

"Love? I'm not sure what that means at the present. I loved my uncle and trusted him with a child's belief in those close to him. That nearly got me killed."

"Does she know who you are, or did you go by Max Hughes?"

"Isn't there anything you don't know?" Max spoke in irritation. His alias, like that night, was his alone to enjoy, his little secret from the demanding public of his world. Secret? Ha!

"It's my job—"

"Yeah, yeah," Max interrupted impatiently. "Due to the circumstances, the treason and all, I'm cutting you some slack here, but you're on dangerous ground."

Chuck raised his eyebrows and showed no signs of quaking in his boots. "Crosby Systems is headquartered in Portland, Oregon. If you leave on the nine-twenty flight tonight, you can be there tomorrow morning."

"Why would I do that?"

"To woo the American beauty. It wouldn't be a bad match. She's smart, well-educated and used to moving among the elite of her society."

"In other words, she wouldn't be an embarrassment as my queen," Max cut in dryly.

"She's also compassionate and does more than take part in charity auctions. She volunteers at a clinic called Children's Connection. It's an adoption agency, mostly funded by another family in the area, the Logans." Chuck paused. "The Logans and the Crosby family are enemies, I think. Twenty-eight years ago, two of the sons were best friends, then six-year-old Robbie Logan was kidnapped while playing at Danny Crosby's house. His mother was supposed to have been watching them."

"The year before Ivy was born," Max said, combining what she'd told him with Chuck's information.

"Yes. The families are also rivals in the high-tech-systems business world."

"You have been busy," Max murmured.

"Once the conspirators were behind bars, I had time to check out…other things."

"Like my wild, passionate night with the rose." Max gave his friend a sardonic glance. "Have you booked my reservation on the nine-twenty flight?"

"Well, I did take the liberty of reserving a seat for you. And alerting Ned to pack a bag."

Max exhaled heavily. "Are you coming, too?"

"If you like. Someone has to, but it can be another security agent, if you prefer."

Max laid a hand on his friend's shoulder. "You'll do. Who, besides Ned, knows me better?"

"Are we going as prince and bodyguard?"

"This isn't an official visit, else I'd have to contact the White House, then the press would be all over us. Let's go as Max Hughes and Chuck Curland. We're consultants on the educational system Crosby is planning for the country."

"Fine by me."

Another worry came to Max. "I've never investigated a woman with an eye toward her being my queen. You have any suggestions?"

Chuck stared at him for a full fifteen seconds, then burst into guffaws.

"If you weren't my friend and security advisor, I'd have you thrown in irons for that," Max told him, becoming somewhat irritated at the joke he didn't get.

Chuck laughed harder. Finally he clamped an arm around Max's shoulders and said in a conspiratorial whisper, "Try flowers. That usually works when courting a woman."

"This is not a courtship," Max informed the American coolly. "This is business."

Three

Friday night Ivy stood near the door of the recreation room located in Children's Connection annex. The combination adoption agency/fertility clinic was holding a bazaar to raise money for new equipment.

"Hey, Ivy," a masculine voice called.

She turned and smiled warmly at the handsome widower who caused no flutters in her heart whatsoever. His hair was blond and sun-streaked, but his eyes were brown, like those of another man who *had* made her heart flutter.

"Hunter, hello," she said. "I was wondering when my cohost for the big event was going to show up."

"Sorry to be late. You know the life of a rancher. If it isn't one thing, it's another." His complaining words were belied by the humor in his eyes. His face became somber. "Actually, Johnny wasn't feeling well. I was a little worried about leaving him with a sitter."

"A late-summer cold?" she asked.

"I don't think so. He seems…tired. Not the usual bundle of energy four-year-olds normally are."

Ivy frowned. "We haven't had any cases of West Nile virus around here, have we?"

"Not that I know of," Hunter replied.

"Nor me," Morgan Davis, director of the adoption agency, said, stopping beside Ivy. His new wife was at his side, looking radiantly happy. There was a contented aura surrounding Morgan, too.

"Oh, hi, you two." Ivy hugged the other couple. Emma, a children's counselor, had been her best friend since college days. Ivy was so glad the other woman had found happiness after her first husband had run out on her.

Emma had been pretty down on life for a while. She'd had two miscarriages during her marriage, then she'd gone through the divorce, then she'd lost her job. Thank God Morgan had offered her a position helping him with the summer camp for older kids who hadn't been adopted. It had given them a chance to get to know each other…and to fall in love.

The two men, who had met when the rancher had adopted his little boy through the agency, shook hands. Emma and Hunter exchanged greetings.

"Em, are you coming to help with the babies tomorrow morning?" Ivy asked after the foursome had chatted awhile.

"Uh, I'm not sure," she said, and cast her husband a worried glance.

Morgan dropped an arm around his wife's shoulders. "I'm trying to get her to slow down," he said with a quiet smile. "Given her history, we think it would be better if she curtailed her activities for a few months."

Ivy knew the couple was trying to start a family. "I understand."

She had news of her own, but she refrained from saying anything since they were in company and might be overheard. She needed to ask Em's advice on what she should do. More and more, that night with Max seemed unreal, the product of a fevered brain.

"We only have three new babies this week," she told Emma when her friend apologized for not helping.

"Are you talking about the adoptive babies here at the agency?" Hunter asked.

"No, at the hospital nursery. We're rocking them." Ivy shook her head sadly. "We have two more crack babies going through drug withdrawal. If we rock and cuddle them almost continuously during the early months, they stand a much better chance of being normal kids."

Nancy Allen, an E.R. nurse from Portland General, stopped near them. "The more rocking, the better," she said, nodding in agreement to Ivy's observation.

Ivy introduced the nurse. "Nancy also volunteers at the nursery. Once we took turns rocking a crying baby for twenty hours straight. All of us, including the baby, got about two hours' sleep during the whole ordeal."

"Now that child is a healthy one-year-old and already walking," Nancy reported. "By the way, I assume everyone knows Everett Baker."

She took the hand of the man who stood a couple of steps behind her and urged him into the group circle. Ivy recognized him as the accountant of Children's Connection, a shy man with dark hair and eyes, about five-ten, same age as Hunter and Morgan, in his midthirties.

Although she'd seen him around the agency during the past six months, she couldn't remember ever doing more than nod as they passed in the corridors.

The men shook hands while the women smiled and murmured in welcome to the newcomer.

"Are the crack babies hard to place?" Everett asked.

Morgan nodded. "The hardest," he admitted. "We have to tell the adoptive parents of the problems they may face."

The accountant looked interested. "Like what?"

Everett brushed his hair off his forehead as he spoke, a nervous gesture, Ivy thought, recalling she'd seen him do it at other times.

"Emotional instability, for one," Morgan said.

"Sometimes mental retardation," Nancy added with pity in her hazel eyes.

"Sometimes," Morgan agreed, "but the biggest problem seems to be the attention-deficit syndrome.

That gets them into trouble in school and adds to their disadvantages."

"So, prospective parents, knowing about the drugs, don't want these babies?" Everett brushed the hair aside again.

Morgan nodded. "Sadly, yes."

Hunter spoke up. "I can identify with that. It's hard enough being a parent without taking on more problems. But what happens to these kids if nobody takes them?"

Ivy felt sorry for Morgan, who as director had to make the hard decisions about these children. A fierce surge of maternal concern flooded her body, causing her to cross her arms over her waist in a protective gesture.

Morgan shrugged. "The usual. Foster homes under the overworked guidance of the city social services unit—out on the street and on their own when they turn eighteen, unless they're hopelessly retarded, in which case it's institutions or group homes."

"That seems so heartless," Ivy murmured.

Emma and the nurse both nodded.

"Sometimes people will take any child, no questions asked, just to get one," Everett said. "Older couples. Desperate ones."

"Not from this agency," Morgan declared firmly. "Nasty surprises for unsuspecting adoptive parents are not in the best interests of the children, not in the long run."

For some reason, Ivy looked back at Everett to see how he would rebut this statement. When the accountant realized everyone was looking at him, he dropped his gaze to the floor and shrugged in an embarrassed manner.

A thought came to Ivy and she spoke without considering the words. "Were you adopted, Everett?"

He visibly jerked, then shook his head in vigorous denial. "No, not me. I was never adopted."

She wondered if he wished he had been and thought his home life might have been difficult. Perhaps he'd had alcoholic parents. Or abusive ones. More likely they were accountants or librarians or something, considering how quiet and reserved he was.

She nodded and smiled, then glanced at Hunter. "I suppose, since we're the hosts, we should circulate and thank everyone for coming out and buying stuff they don't need so this event will be a success."

"I have this theory about charity sales and such," Morgan said in a cheerful manner, sweeping a hand out to include the tables piled high with brownies, cakes, aprons, pot holders and other goodies on sale. "It goes along with the fruitcake theory."

Ivy played the straight man. "What's that?"

"There are at most only ten fruitcakes and they get circulated around the country at Christmas," he explained. "The donated stuff we have here gets sold again and again at different bazaars until it's circulated all over town, probably once every five or ten years."

"Yeah," Hunter said with great seriousness, but a

twinkle in his eyes, "that sounds about right. A friend and I kept up with the ugliest urn we ever saw at a church fund-raiser one time. That was the second time it had been there that we personally knew of. Sure enough, it turned up again at the same church three years later, then six or seven years after that I saw it at another charity event. I felt so bad about the poor thing, I bought it for my grandmother. It's still at the ranch with roses growing all over it so nobody can see it."

Ivy laughed with the others at this happy-ending tale, then she and Hunter roamed from table to table and thanked the donors and the buyers for taking part.

By the time they helped close the place down, it was almost midnight. Driving home through the pleasantly cool September night, she realized she was tired. It wasn't something she usually noticed. She tended to keep going until the job was finished.

Tomorrow she would sleep until eight, then head for the hospital to cuddle the two crack babies for three hours, then she was to meet her sister for lunch.

A shiver slid down her back. Should she tell Katie about the pregnancy? Yes. It would become self-evident in a short time, so there was no need for secrecy, especially with her family.

Not that her father or mother would notice until she hit them over the head with it, so to speak. Jack and his second wife, Toni, once his assistant at the office, hung out with the retired golf-and-country-club set. Sheila, Ivy's mother, had her own crowd and spent part of the year in Palm Springs. She often returned to Portland with a new youthful look, thanks to spas and the skill of the plastic surgeons in southern California.

When she got home, Ivy poured a glass of low-fat milk and ate a banana before heading for bed. She figured she should start eating regularly instead of forgetting herself in work. Also, she should eat healthier foods and cut back on the jalapeño peppers she loved. Probably they were bad for the baby.

For a moment, she experienced a lowering of her spirits as she realized just how little she knew about babies and prenatal care.

A baby. Oh, heavens!

Max, where are you when I need you?

"Max Hughes," she said aloud. "That's the man I mean, not the prince."

But, she realized, that man—Max Hughes, the wonderful companion-friend-lover—had never existed.

No matter. She had her siblings, Katie and Trent, Danny, too, although their younger brother was mostly a recluse in Hawaii. She had friends such as Emma and her new husband. All these would provide family and role models for her child.

Her spirits rebounded a bit.

"I just hate for babies to be hurt," Nancy Allen said when Ivy entered the nursery the next morning promptly at nine. The E.R. nurse held two tiny, squalling tots, one on her shoulder and the other lying prone in her lap. Her short brown hair swung out around her face as she shook her head in disgust.

Ivy took the baby from the other woman's lap and, crooning softly, settled in a rocking chair and cuddled it close as she rocked and hummed to it. After fifteen minutes, the baby girl settled down. When she tried to get her fist to her mouth, Ivy helped her get it in place. The child sucked contentedly and dozed off.

Nancy got the baby she held to sleep, laid him in the rolling bassinet and lifted a ten-month-old baby who was staring fretfully at the ceiling. Like Ivy, she cuddled the infant and hummed, then played patty-cake and other games to engage the youngster's interest and get it to interact with people.

"I read that there seems to be a link between autism and allergies to wheat and/or dairy products," Nancy said in a low tone when both babies were asleep.

Ivy nodded. "I saw the article, too. Also that some immunization shots might be a factor."

"I know that some people are against any genetic alterations, but if we could identify and correct these problems before the child spends a lifetime in misery, wouldn't that be better?"

"It would seem so," Ivy said honestly. "It seems a shame not to help those we can. But what do you do with parents who want their child to be a genius or tall enough to be a basketball player?"

"That's where the problem comes in," Nancy agreed. "Where do we draw the line?"

The door to the nursery opened and Everett Baker

came in, looking a bit sheepish. "Uh, I thought I would see if I could, uh, help." He brushed the stubborn lock off his forehead and looked as if he might bolt at a harsh word.

"Of course you can," Nancy told him. "Sit right here. I'll get you a baby." She went into the adjacent room.

Ivy smiled warmly as Everett took the rocking chair. He smiled back, then looked at the floor. Bashful. Poor guy.

"Here you are." Nancy bustled in with a sleepy baby wrapped in pink. "Isn't she adorable?"

Ivy saw the nurse had given Everett one of the "good" babies, one who smiled and cooed at the slightest encouragement. In for some tests, she was due to go home with her parents on Monday.

"Yeah," he said, staring at the child with an uncertain expression.

Nancy grinned at Ivy, then showed him how to hold the baby on his lap so she could look into his face. "Smile at her," she ordered.

Everett did. The baby gave a big, drooly smile back. He looked amusingly surprised at the response. His shoulders relaxed and his smile became real.

"See? She likes you," Nancy said, beaming. She checked the schedule, then prepared bottles for Ivy's and Everett's two, then one for a third baby, whom she brought into the comforting room, as they called it.

Together the three rocked and fed the infants. The only sound was the whisper of the filtered air from the overhead vents and the sucking noises of three little rosebud mouths. Ivy sighed contentedly.

As soon as Everett's little girl was finished, he rose from the chair. "I've got to go."

"Put the baby in her crib in the other room," Nancy directed. "Thanks for coming by. That was a big help."

He followed directions, then hastily left.

"What is it about teeny little babies that frightens grown men out of their wits?" she demanded.

The two women laughed. Ivy wondered how Max would be with children. Would he be at ease with them? Would he hold their child? Talk and play silly games to socialize him or her?

A playboy prince interested in home and hearth? She wished.

Pain sliced right through her middle, cutting her heart in two. How could she have been so stupid?

"Ivy! How could you have been so careless?" Katie demanded, her eyebrows rising in shock behind her glasses. She hooked a lock of thick, sun-kissed hair behind her ear.

"I know," Ivy said, admitting to the madness of the moment. "I don't understand it myself."

The two women were sitting on Ivy's patio, eating chicken-salad-stuffed tomatoes. Katie was on a diet—she'd already lost over thirty pounds—and Ivy didn't want to ruin her efforts. They idly watched golfers tee off at the fifteenth hole while joggers loped along the trail next to the creek.

"Are you thinking of abortion?"

Ivy shook her head adamantly. "I want the baby, although I do wonder if I'm being selfish in having it and not providing a father."

"Do you think, if he knew, he would want marriage?"

Ivy shook her head again.

"It's his child, too," Katie reminded her, a ring of indignation in the words. "Men should take responsibility for their families."

To her horror, tears flooded Ivy's eyes.

"Oh, honey, I didn't mean to make you feel bad." Katie patted her arm and looked concerned. "Tell the father. He should know."

"He might not want to know," Ivy admitted grimly. "Why would a globe-trotting prince, soon to be king, care about the result of a one-night stand?"

"Prince, king, playboy, whatever, he's the father," Katie said firmly. "If you can't bring yourself to contact him, I certainly have no qualms about it."

"Oh, no, please don't! Not yet," Ivy added in a calmer tone. "I have a doctor's appointment next week. Just to be sure. Then I'll…maybe I'll call him."

Hi, Max, it's your one-night stand. Guess what?

Maybe he wouldn't even remember her.

Hello, Max. It's Ivy.

Ivy who?

The dreadful scenarios played out in her mind like snippets from a horror movie. "I have to think about it," she now said to her sister. "When I'm sure."

"Whatever you want to do about the baby, I'm behind you a hundred percent."

"Thanks. I'm okay," Ivy insisted, blinking foolish tears away. She felt young and stupid in comparison to Katie's calm manner.

Only a year older than Ivy, Katie was vice president of research and development at Crosby Systems. She had a degree from Stanford University. Everyone knew she was a "brain."

Ivy had tried to pattern herself after her older sister so that she would be seen as more than the baby of the family. So, here she was, single and pregnant. She hated to bring gossip down on her siblings.

There was also the question of what her parents were going to say. She could imagine her mother's fury. Sheila liked to cause all the scandal in the family—

Ivy broke the traitorous thought. *She* was the one in trouble here. She'd better concentrate on that.

"You cut your hair," Katie suddenly said. "I just realized you don't have it up in a ponytail the way you usually do. It's gone!"

"I…I was tired of it."

Don't ever cut your hair, Max had said in an imperious voice, running his hands through the wavy mass and fanning it out on the pillow.

Just before they made love for the third time.

She managed to stifle the groan that nearly escaped her. Going in for a haircut the other day, she'd impulsively told the stylist to cut it all off.

"I like it short," Katie said with a smile. "You look like a mischievous cherub with all those golden curls around your face and those big blue eyes."

This time Ivy did groan. "That's exactly what I was aiming for," she muttered sarcastically.

Her sister yawned and stood. "I have reports to read before a meeting on Monday. Take care of yourself. Don't worry about anything. Trent and I will be here for you. You know that, don't you?"

"Thanks, Katie. No wonder you're my favorite sister."

"I'm your only sister," Katie dutifully reminded her.

This was an old joke, stemming from a time when nine-year-old Ivy had told ten-year-old Katie she was her least favorite sister. Katie had taunted her by saying, "I'm your *only* sister, dummy, so that makes me your favorite, too."

"Does not!"

"Does so!"

"Does not!"

Their mother had broken up the argument by telling them to shut up, she had a headache.

The fight had ended with the girls sticking their tongues out at each other and crossing their eyes, then dissolving into laughter, quickly stifled with pillows so their mother wouldn't ground them for the weekend.

Ivy walked Katie to the door and hugged her as they said their farewells. "Come have lunch with me tomorrow?" Katie invited.

"I have some catching up on work to do, too. I'll be writing up notes on the laptop."

"All work and no play," Katie warned.

"Huh. Everyone knows who the workaholics in

the family are. Danny and I just doodle at writing programs while you and Trent keep the contracts coming in."

After affectionate smiles and a heartfelt goodbye, Ivy returned to the patio and settled into her chair with a loud sigh. It was hard to keep up the pretense that she had everything under control when she really felt she was on the proverbial slippery slope and rapidly gaining speed on the way down.

She did some work, then read several business magazines before deciding she needed to get in some exercise as part of her new health-conscious program. Once in jogging shorts, matching top and jogging shoes, she headed across the lawn and down to the creek in the arroyo. The path ran along its banks under alder, maple and cottonwood trees.

September. By the end of the month, the leaves would be showing tinges of fall color. Gold. Scarlet. Russet.

Winter would come and with it, the rain. People rarely carried umbrellas here unless it was a real downpour. But she would, for the baby's sake.

Then it would be spring. The baby would be due in April, along with the tulips and daffodils. She would name the baby after a flower. Or the month. April, that was a pretty name. Perhaps Katherine for her sister.

April Katherine? Katherine April?

Arriving at the path, she continued to think about the baby as she started a slow warm-up run. It occurred to her that she was assuming the child was a girl.

She sighed and stopped to do some light stretches at the half-mile marker. Girls are easier to raise, she decided as she touched her fingers to her toes.

On the other hand, boys didn't get pregnant.

If her son got a girl pregnant, she would throttle him, then escort him and the girl to the minister. No child of hers would disavow a child....

Please, she ordered her wildly roaming mind, one problem at a time. Let's get this baby here before we start worrying about grandchildren.

"Watch out!"

She glanced up in time to see a golf ball come whizzing right at her. She ducked and it went flying over her head to plunk against a tree, then roll down the path and stop against her shoe.

Two men rushed down the slope from the golf course. "I'm terribly sorry," one of them called. "I sliced, and the ball hit a tree, then came flying your way."

"That's okay. No harm done," Ivy assured the two older men, who were panting from their run. She picked up the ball and tossed it across the narrow creek to them. "Have a good game."

"Thanks," the men said in unison and trudged up the hill to the fairway.

Ivy stretched her arms over her head, reaching for the sky. She started when she spied two other men standing at the bend in the trail ahead, observing her intently.

A shiver danced along her scalp and down her

spine. The two men were the same height. They had identical lean, muscular builds. One's hair was lighter, though, with sun streaks running through the brown. The other's was as black as midnight. The dappled sunlight cast diamond dust over it as the leaves shifted above his head. His dark gaze never strayed from her face.

She gasped. Blinked. Gasped again.

Thankfully the world started to rapidly go dark. She grabbed the post supporting the chin-up bar, then felt her right knee sink into the soft mulch of the path. Forcing her eyes open, she saw she was going down like a ship with a slow leak.

"She's fainting," a man's voice said close by.

Well, duh, she thought, pressing one hand against the ground to stop the downward spiral.

"I've got her," another said.

She was lifted into strong arms as if she weighed no more than a sack of sugar.

"Can you hear me?" the man holding her asked.

She opened her eyes and focused with difficulty. "Put me down. I can walk," she said coolly, furiously.

"She's glad to see me," Max said to his companion, ironic amusement overlaying his deep baritone.

"I can tell," his friend replied.

Ivy closed her eyes, hoping when she opened them that none of this would be happening….

Four

"That's a steep hill," Ivy heard the other man say. "Let's make a packsaddle to carry her up. Her apartment is the one on this end of the nearest building."

Ivy opened her eyes and struggled to be free. "I'm fine. I can walk."

Max let her feet slip to the ground, but he kept her in a protective embrace. "The hospital is closer."

"Good idea," his friend said.

"It isn't a good idea," Ivy informed them. She groaned and put a hand to her head as dizziness attacked her, belying her words.

"Let's go," Max said. "I'll carry you if I have to," he warned when she balked. He turned back to the path, his arm around her waist.

"I don't need to see a doctor. And I don't need

you," she said, desperate to get away from him and get herself composed and used—resigned?—to the idea of Max being here in Portland. "What are you doing here, anyway?"

"Looking for you," he replied in his wonderfully smooth voice. "Why else?" He gently turned her again and headed for her apartment complex.

"Oh." She couldn't think of another word. They started up the grassy hill. She glanced at the other man and found him surveying the area as if thinking of buying it or else looking for a mugger behind every tree. "Who are you?"

"A friend," Max said. "Charles Curland. Chuck and I went to school together. Brown University," he added before she could ask.

"Glad to meet you," the friend said politely.

From the laughter in his eyes, she thought he was about to become hysterical with delight. "My pleasure," she responded automatically, her tone full of doubt.

The man cast her a knowing glance, then grinned. There was something open and very likable about him. Her gaze went to Max. *Prince Regent Max.* Huh. Too bad she couldn't detect the same traits in him!

Although she tried to ignore it, she was acutely aware of his arm around her waist, of the strength and warmth of his body as he walked next to her. She wanted to lay her head on his shoulder and let him take the burden of an unplanned pregnancy from her.

A gasp escaped her at the ridiculous idea. Then

the awful dizziness flashed over her again, and she had to lean into him to keep from swaying.

"We're almost there," he murmured in the same dulcet tones she recalled from that night.

They strode up the sidewalk, the three steps to her porch, and stopped at her door.

"The key," Max said.

"It isn't locked."

He gave her a stern glance before opening the door and ushering her inside. His dark eyes took in the whole living area at a glance, then he led her to the sofa and with a gentle but firm touch laid her upon it.

"I'm fine," she said, smiling brightly to prove it. "You can go now." She pushed herself upright in the corner of the sofa.

"What is the number of your doctor?" he asked.

"It's Saturday. His day off," she added, when the day of the week didn't seem to make an impression.

"He will see you," Max asserted.

At last anger came to her aid. "This isn't Lantanya, Your Highness or Majesty or whatever you call yourself. You have no authority here."

He studied her with a gaze so sharp she felt it right inside her. It made her nervous. She crossed her arms over her middle so he couldn't detect the child growing there.

"So you know," he said in an oddly quiet, thoughtful manner, as if he regretted the fact.

"I saw it in a tabloid. Along with a picture of us going into the resort."

A blush started at her toes and rushed up to her

face like a wildfire through a dry forest. She glanced at his friend and saw compassion in his gaze. Pressing her lips together, she stared miserably at the floor, feeling foolish and deceived and gullible.

All of which she had certainly been in July.

"Chuck is also my security advisor," Max told her. "He knows everything." He paused. "Everything," he murmured in a low, husky tone.

The heat swept over her again. She leaped from the sofa and headed to the powder room down the hall past the kitchen. "I have to—I'm going to—"

She clamped a hand over her mouth.

Max followed her into the tiny bathroom. He held her head while she was violently ill. She didn't know whether she was going to die from the nausea or embarrassment. At the moment she didn't much care which it was. She just hoped it would happen soon.

In a bizarre repeat of that magical night, he dampened a washcloth and ministered to her, ignoring her protests as he had nearly two months ago. He wiped her face and down her neck, then stood close while she used mouthwash, all the while wishing she could disappear in a wisp of smoke.

"I'm fine," she said in a near whisper, yet feeling weak and shaky and terribly unsure of herself.

Grabbing a comb, she tried to bestow some order to her riotous curls. Her elbow bumped him in the chest. The room was much too small for both of them.

She tossed the comb in a drawer, refusing to look at him or herself in the mirror. "I'm really okay."

"Yeah, right," Max said. He touched a curl. "I liked your hair long—"

"It was too much trouble," she said, defending her decision to have it cut.

"But," he continued, "I also like it this way. It suits you, I think."

"Oh."

He inched closer, then encircled her with his arms and laid both hands on her abdomen. "Is there a child?"

Startled, she met his eyes in the gilt mirror she'd found beside the Dumpster behind her building and had rescued and restored to its original beauty. The glass seemed to go hazy, then it began to darken.

"Not again," she said in equal parts disgust and despair.

Max's arms tightened around her as she held the edge of the counter. Then she slipped into blissful oblivion.

"Chuck!" Max called. "I need some help."

Chuck appeared at the door. His eyebrows rose in amusement as he helped Max get the unconscious Ivy into the living room again. "You do have a way with women," he murmured, stepping back as Max bent over Ivy.

"Should we call an ambulance?" Max wanted to know, his insides clenched into knots as he studied Ivy's still figure. "I think there's a baby. Could she be miscarrying?"

Guilt at surprising her—shocking her, he

amended—hit him deep and hard. He stared at her beautiful face, which looked like that of a cherub with its frame of golden curls. He groaned silently as desire mingled with the prickling of his conscience.

Chuck looked worried now. "That's her car in the parking space outside. Let's use it and take her to the emergency room. That will be the quickest."

Max nodded. He needed action. "Find the keys. I'll take care of her."

Chuck went to the purse on the kitchen counter and removed a set of keys. "Got 'em. Let's go."

Max carried Ivy while Chuck opened and closed doors. In a couple of minutes they were off. They used the frontage road to the hospital instead of going on the freeway, and in less than five minutes pulled up at the emergency entrance to the hospital. An orderly brought a gurney out when he saw them lifting the unconscious woman from the car.

"Accident?" he asked.

"No. She fainted," Max said. "Twice."

The man wheeled her into the emergency room.

Another nurse joined them. "That's Ivy Crosby," she said. "I was with her this morning in the nursery. What happened?" Her hazel eyes darted between Max and Chuck as if suspicious of them.

"She fainted," Max said again, beginning to feel he was going to do something desperate if the E.R. staff didn't stop asking questions and start treatment. "I thought…she could be miscarrying."

"I'll get help," the orderly said and left them to go

to a phone at the receptionist's desk. "Can one of you sign her in?"

"I will," Max said impatiently. "Where's a doctor?"

"On his way," the cheerful orderly said a few seconds later. "We'll put her in a room."

Max and Chuck followed the others through swinging doors that said No Admittance and into a cubicle. The nurse already had a chart in hand and began filling in blanks as she took Ivy's vital signs. She hooked up monitors and soon the steady blip of a heartbeat appeared on a screen.

Ivy opened her eyes. "I want to go home."

Max took her hand. "Not until the doctor sees you."

"That would be me," the doctor said, coming into the cubicle. "Ivy is my patient. Hi, what have you done to yourself?" he asked her.

Max didn't like the casual manner of the entire E.R. personnel. "She fainted," he said for the umpteenth time. "She's…she may be pregnant, so there could be a problem."

An odd feeling pierced his chest. He realized he felt the possible loss of the child as a physical thing—an actual ache in his heart.

"Is that so?" the doctor said, peering at Ivy.

"I have an appointment with you next week," she said, not looking at Max. "I, uh, got a test kit earlier this week. It was positive."

The doctor, who looked pretty young to Max, turned to the men. He wasn't wearing a wedding ring, Max noted.

"If you gentlemen will excuse us?" he said.

The orderly ushered them into a waiting room to the right of the E.R. reception area. "I'll call you when she's ready," he said and disappeared.

"Ready for what?" Max demanded irritably. He hadn't liked being tossed out of the cubicle. If he'd been her husband, they wouldn't have thrown him out.

But he wasn't.

"We have to be married right away," he said to Chuck.

Chuck's eyebrows rose sardonically. "No, thanks. It isn't that I don't like you, but not that way."

If looks could kill, Max would have sizzled his friend into a cinder in ten seconds.

Chuck smiled slightly. "She's in good hands. Her water hasn't broken so I don't think there's a miscarriage. I also think part of her fainting was that she didn't want to face you, old man."

Max stilled at this diagnosis. He considered it from several angles. One reason Chuck was his best friend was that the man told him the truth as he saw it. Max hoped he was right about the child being okay.

"You think she's afraid of me," he concluded after mulling over the second part of Chuck's observations. "Why?"

Chuck went over to the coffeemaker and poured them each a plastic cup of the strong brew. He returned to his chair and handed one cup to Max. "She doesn't know what you want from her. Maybe she's worried you'll try to take the baby when it comes. Mothers can be pretty protective."

"Hmm." Max paced the narrow space between the sofa and the table where the coffee setup was located. "Pregnant women can be pretty unreasonable." He saw his friend's quickly concealed surprise. "Or so I've read," he muttered, frowning to cover the disturbing swirl of emotion that ran over him at the thought of Ivy carrying his child.

Chuck nodded. "She seems rather independent. She also didn't seem interested in the fact that you're of a royal family. How are you going to convince her to marry you and return to Lantanya?"

Leave it to Chuck to state what Max hadn't wanted to admit. His passionate rose may have literally fallen at his feet, but she wasn't the woman he'd kissed and made love to.

The blood boiled through his veins at the thought of that night. He couldn't remember the last occasion he'd made love three times in one night with a woman. When he'd run out of condoms after the second time, he'd knowingly taken a chance, unable to resist the passion that rode him with a relentless demand for completion.

It had been the same for her, he recalled, unable to suppress a smile as he recalled the pleasures in her lips, her arms, her supple body, the way she'd touched him and clung to him….

"Earth to Max."

He glanced at Chuck. "What?"

"The doctor."

The doctor entered the small waiting room, his smile meant to be reassuring. Max wanted the man to tell him what he needed to hear.

The doctor removed the stethoscope from around his neck and slipped it into the pocket of his white jacket. "She's doing fine."

"So she insisted just before she fainted a second time," Max said.

"Hormones," the doctor said casually. "And surprise. She said she hadn't expected to see you."

"Obviously."

It occurred to Max that Ivy didn't want to see him, that she hadn't intended to contact him about the child. Had their night together meant so little?

Something hard and painful coalesced inside him. Was she, like his uncle, playing some game of her own?

He would find out. Neither his kingdom, his heir nor his heart was up for grabs. Not by anyone, not even the rose.

Ivy Crosby appeared composed while she gave her insurance information to the E.R. receptionist. Nancy Allen returned Ivy's smile when she thanked her and the orderly for their help. When the tall, dark-haired man took her arm and escorted her outside, she went docilely.

Nancy thought the man's actions were rather romantic. She continued her duties, glad she had the day shift and that it wasn't yet busy for a Saturday. After checking supplies and straightening up the cubicle, she went on her break. In the cafeteria, at the tables reserved for the medical staff, she sank into a chair with a cup of tea and idly picked up a newspaper someone had left there.

The headline read The Lion Roars.

Nancy grimaced in disgust. The paper was a weekly tabloid, its articles so wild they couldn't possibly be true. Nevertheless she propped her feet on another chair, sipped the tea and read through the main story.

Ah, a romantic tryst with a prince, who was soon to be king of some place she could just barely recall from long-ago school days. She glanced at the accompanying picture.

Then looked again.

Holding the grainy print nearly to her nose, she studied the pair. "My gosh," she murmured. "My gosh!"

She removed the front page from the tabloid, folded it into a neat square and tucked it into her pocket. This was exciting news, and she couldn't wait to tell it to someone.

At that moment, Everett Baker, the accountant she'd been sort of seeing of late, entered the cafeteria. His face brightened at seeing her and he came over.

"Hi," she said, glad to see him, too. "What are you doing here? It's Saturday."

"Catching up," he told her. "Inputting files into the computer."

"You shouldn't have to do all that work. The adoption agency should hire you more help."

"It isn't in the budget," he explained in his serious manner that she found endearing.

While he got a cup of coffee, she refreshed her tea and settled at the table again. There were few other people in the place as afternoon visiting hours were over and the evening hours hadn't started.

When Everett returned, she removed the tabloid page and handed it to him. "Guess who I just saw?"

Looking mystified, Everett unfolded the page and glanced over the headlines of the stories.

"Look at the picture with the main story," Nancy urged. "Do you recognize anyone?"

He shook his head.

She laughed softly. "That's Ivy Crosby with the prince. Guess what?"

He brought the picture closer to his face and studied it. "What?"

"They were just in the E.R." When he gave her a puzzled stare, she added, "The prince—that man in the photo—and Ivy Crosby. Here. In Portland. At this hospital."

"Were they in an accident?"

"No. She fainted. Twice, the prince said." Nancy lofted her eyebrows in a significant manner.

Everett looked concerned. "West Nile virus?"

Nancy rolled her eyes. Men could be so obtuse. She leaned close although there was no one around to hear. "She's pregnant. You can't tell anyone. Swear."

"Uh, I swear."

She sighed. "He was so worried about her."

"The prince?"

"Of course the prince," Nancy said, somewhat exasperated. She smiled in apology when Everett glanced at her in surprise and brushed the hair off his forehead.

"Sorry," he said. "I have…things on my mind."

"Come have dinner at my place," she invited on an impulse. "I'll pick up a roasted chicken at the grocery, so it'll be quick and easy."

"That would be nice. Should I bring some wine?"

"A white wine would be perfect." She beamed at him, then took the tabloid page back and returned it to her pocket. "Do you think they'll get married?"

Everett shrugged. He wasn't interested in some foreign prince and his troubles. He had enough worries of his own. His associates were putting pressure on him to come up with additional babies for their purposes.

That was why he was working on the weekend, searching through the records of the foolish girls who'd gotten themselves in trouble and had recently come to the clinic for help. If the Stork could get to them first, he could usually convince them—for a price—to sign the coming baby over to him. Then he would sell the child on the black market for big bucks. There were couples who would pay any price and ask no questions.

"Speaking of babies," he said, trying to sound casual, "how are the crack babies doing?"

Nancy sighed and looked troubled. "I don't know what's going to happen to them. The mothers are refusing to give them up for adoption, yet how can they take care of their babies? They can't take care of themselves."

Her tendency to gossip was the first thing that had drawn him to her. He'd wanted information about the babies. More babies meant more money, and he was determined to be rich someday. But the other thing that kept him coming around was her compassion, he reluctantly admitted. She was a caring person and would make a good mother.

A scene, like one from a movie, flashed into his mind, so clear it was as if he was there....

"Open it, darling." The woman, dressed in a blue fleecy robe, had urged the boy. One other person had been in the room—a man who was the father.

"I know what it is," the boy declared, his smile splitting his face from ear to ear.

A Christmas tree stood before a big window in the large but comfortable room. Under it, presents beckoned in brightly wrapped packages. A fire burned in the brick-lined fireplace. It was like a scene from a calendar.

"Are you going to open it, or are you going to shake it to death?" the father demanded, his manner teasing.

The boy tore off the wrappings and lifted a baseball mitt from the box. "Oh, boy!" he said. "This is perfect! Wait'll I show Danny. I hope he got one, too. That way we can practice every day."

The happy little family laughed as they continued to open gifts and exclaim over them....

Everett pressed a hand to his chest as a sudden heaviness settled there, as if someone had rolled a boulder on top of him. The pressure made him want to cry. He sternly brought his mind back to the problem at hand—finding out more about drug babies that no one wanted.

"Everett, what is it?" Nancy asked. "You look so sad."

"Uh, I was thinking about how hard life must be for the crack children, especially those who aren't adopted and don't get help when they're little."

She touched his arm, warming him with the compassionate smile on her face. The nurse was pretty with her short brown hair and hazel eyes. He liked her.

But that was all, he reminded the part of him that was attracted to her. He was a man. A physical attraction was normal and didn't mean anything special.

"Well," she said, "I've got another two hours. Come over around seven, okay?"

He nodded and watched her walk away, her steps brisk as she returned to duty. She was nice. He wondered why that meant so much to him.

Two hours later, at his apartment, he showered and changed into dark slacks and a white shirt. He picked up a bottle of chilled white wine at the grocery and went over to Nancy's place.

His heart thumped when she opened the door. Her smile was welcoming, very welcoming. There were flowers and candles on a small table, which was already set for two.

"Do come in," she invited. "Brr, it's already getting cold at night, isn't it?" She closed the door when he stepped inside.

Her graciousness reminded him of the family scene he'd imagined earlier. She was like the woman in it—warm and loving, bestowing happiness on those around her.

The heaviness invaded his chest again. As if he were a child, the need to cry pushed against his control. He forced a smile and handed Nancy the wine. One thing about having Joleen Baker for a mother, he'd learned self-discipline at an early age. If he cried, she slapped him to "give him something to cry about." He learned to control his emotions.

"This is perfect," Nancy said of the wine. "The corkscrew is on the counter. Would you open it?"

"Sure." He went into the tiny kitchen and opened the bottle while she removed the chicken from the oven where it was keeping warm.

He accidentally brushed her hip as they both started for the table. Heat, sweet, gentle and compelling, warmed his insides and eased the odd heaviness.

"That's better," she said, looking him over after she placed a platter of chicken, potatoes and carrots on the table. "That smile is real." She shook her head. "I don't think I've ever known a truly shy man before."

Funny, but he hadn't even realized he was smiling. "You're easy to be around," he told Nancy.

They talked about their childhood memories over

the meal. Everett admitted to moving around a lot. "My parents drank," he said, not meaning to say that at all.

She nodded. "I thought it was something like that. At times I've sensed a sadness in you that touches my heart. Perhaps you need to establish a family of your own, one that'll be happy and all."

Nancy's thoughtful gaze reminded him of the woman. She'd had dark-blond hair with reddish highlights in it. Her eyes had been brown and seemed to see into the boy's young soul just the way this woman seemed to peer into his.

"I'm perfectly content," he said a little coolly, drawing back from that feminine warmth. Joleen had sometimes been nice, too, then suddenly she would turn on him and be a bitch. A man had to be careful around others.

"Do you like your job?" Nancy asked him.

"Yes. Do you?"

"I love it." Her radiant smile indicated she truly did.

"Why?" he asked, curious about her, needing to understand the kindness she so freely extended to others.

"I like people," she said after a moment of consideration. "I am a little nosy." She wrinkled her nose at him, then laughed. "But not in a mean way. I like knowing what makes others tick, why they do the things they do."

"Maybe you should have gone into the psychiatric field, since you have a penchant for understanding people."

"Maybe." She hesitated. "I'd like to understand you…for instance, what makes you so sad at times. The look in your eyes when you came to the nursery this morning made me want to cry."

He frowned, not liking the thought of anyone seeing that far into him. Being vulnerable was something he'd learned early to guard against. "You're imagining a lot more than I was feeling," he told her.

"You felt sorry for the babies," she told him softly but firmly.

As if she knew him better than he knew himself! He grimaced. "Children don't have choices," he said with an edge of bitterness he couldn't hide. "Adults hold all the cards."

"What was your home life like?"

"Which part do you mean? The alcoholic mother? Or the father who abandoned us?"

"Oh, Everett, I'm so sorry," she murmured, a stricken expression on her face.

"That was a long time ago. It doesn't matter now."

"It does. It hurts forever."

He didn't argue. Instead he thought of the babies he'd seen in the nursery and the two whose identity he now knew.

Those kids needed care, lots of it, and the Stork knew people who needed babies to complete their lives. Taking them from the nursery would be a snap and a service to all involved. He would make money. The kids would have good homes. As was often said, all's well that ends well.

Five

Ivy sat on the patio and glared at Max. He didn't pay the slightest bit of attention. He was reading the Portland newspaper—*her* newspaper—as if he hadn't a care in the world.

But then, why would he? Kings commanded; others jumped to do their bidding. Chuck Curland had left fast enough when Max had indicated he wanted to be alone with Ivy.

Not that she wanted to be alone with him.

She stared off into space. Since her patio apartment was at the end of the building, she had a clear vista in three directions. The creek, golf course and the hill with the medical complex was to the south.

In the western sky, the last pink and golden tints of the sunset faded as twilight deepened behind the coastal mountain range. Almost due east, Mt. Hood rose to a majestic 11,235 feet, its top swathed in clouds.

Today was still Saturday. Incredible. It seemed a month at the very least since she'd gotten up, visited the babies at the hospital, had lunch with Katie, did some work at her home computer, then had gone for a jog at which time she'd nearly been hit by a golf ball, come face-to-face with Max and gone down in a faint, the first of her entire life.

After they'd returned from the hospital, Max had urged her to lie on the sofa and rest. She'd done so, hoping it would make him leave. Instead he'd checked the refrigerator, then asked his friend to bring them a gallon of milk and several selections of fruit. Once he had the items and Chuck had again departed, Max had prepared omelettes for their dinner along with bowls of fresh fruit salad.

"If your countrymen could see you now," she'd mocked.

He'd merely given her an amused glance. "My father believed in keeping me on a strict allowance during my university days. Chuck was on scholarship. We decided we could save a lot of money by cooking for ourselves. Then we found out we had to learn to cook."

A vivid picture leaped into Ivy's mind. Max holding a match to the pan and lighting the sauce in which the cherries bubbled, then spooning the flaming concoction over the dish of ice cream. She and Max gazing into each other's eyes as they ate the delicious dessert. His kiss when they were finished. His hands roaming over her in passionate delight, touching her in ways no other ever had. The heated pleasure they had shared…

A deeply felt sigh escaped her.

Max—she couldn't think of him as Prince Max—perused her over the top of the paper, then laid it aside. His dark, probing gaze ran over her. "Why the sigh? What are you thinking?" he asked, suddenly leaning close and gazing into her eyes. "Ah, that night."

"No," she choked out, but the flaming of her cheeks gave her away.

His face hardened. "A child came of that night of passion. When were you going to tell me?"

"I don't know."

"You weren't going to notify me, were you?" His voice dropped to a deadly dangerous level.

The fine, chiseled structure of his face seemed to harden while she debated her answer. Whatever else she'd anticipated from this moment, she hadn't expected this raw anger from him, as if she'd tried to cheat him of his rights or something.

"How could I?" she finally asked. "You didn't give me your real name. You let me think you were in Lantanya on business, the same as I was. It was only through a tabloid that I found out who you really are."

He waved that aside. "You left before we had a chance to talk the next morning. Had I been a mere business traveler passing through the area, I might not have been able to trace you. Fortunately, I was aware of Crosby Systems and the work your company was doing."

"Your father negotiated the contract last year before—" She stopped, realizing the death of his father wasn't something she wanted to mention.

Max's face softened fractionally. "It was his dream, and my mother's, that Lantanya would become the best-educated country in the world, all the way through the university level. Now it is my goal, a monument to both of them and their vision."

The faint sound of a siren came to them from the highway, then became louder as the ambulance raced up the hill to the hospital. Although she couldn't see the E.R. portico from her patio, she knew when the vehicle reached its destination because the siren stopped.

"Another emergency," Max said, his eyes narrowing. "That's the third one since we've been sitting out here."

She realized she hadn't noticed the other two. "You're observant."

A slight bitterness tinged his smile. "I've learned to be, especially of late."

"Why?"

He shrugged.

Seeing that he wasn't going to answer, she asked, "What happens next?" She really wanted to know when he was going to leave. She needed to be alone, to think.

"We must marry."

Her hand jerked, making her spill the last swallow of iced tea. She set the tumbler down on the glass-topped table and shook her head.

"We must," he insisted calmly.

His smile unnerved her. He sounded so confident, as if he knew, not only what was best but what was inevitable.

"I… We don't really know each other," she said, a weak argument but the only one she could muster.

"I know you better than any other man ever has."

There was a knowing look in his eyes, and she had put it there. The heat rose in her again. "That was passion," she protested. "One night doesn't count as a lifelong friendship."

"Knowing each other in the biblical sense was a beginning," he calmly stated. "That there is a very real attraction between us as a man and woman bodes well for marriage, don't you think?"

"No! I mean…I don't know what to think." She pressed a hand to her forehead, trying to think things through and not be swayed by his seeming logic.

A frown settled on his handsome face and he studied her for several long seconds. "When were you going to tell me about your condition?"

"I wasn't. That is, I hadn't made up my mind about what to do. I thought, when I saw the doctor, I'd decide."

"Then I showed up and spoiled that plan." He smiled, the humor after the anger surprising her. "What was plan B?"

"I hadn't got that far."

He nodded. "Hormones, as the doctor said," he murmured, giving her a sympathetic look, which confused her and caused her heart to thump against her chest wall.

The phone rang.

"I'll get it." He rose and went inside, returning almost at once. "It's for you."

"Well, duh," she muttered. She took the portable phone and put it to her ear, ignoring Max who sat and leaned close so he could hear, too. She gave him a glare that did no good. "Hello?"

"Ivy!" her sister said.

Ivy prepared herself for bad news. "Hi, Katie. What's happening?"

"I should ask you that. Was that your prince who answered the phone?"

"Uh, yes, well, not exactly." He wasn't *her* prince, only a prince. It was too complicated to explain. "What is it? You sound excited."

"Emma just called. She spoke to her neighbor— they ran into each other at the grocery store—and the neighbor's nephew works in the E.R. at the hospital."

Ivy groaned. She knew what was coming.

"The nephew said you were brought in by two men. He didn't know either of them, but one of them seemed to be in charge and signed the E.R. forms for you. The name he used was Max Hughes. That *is* your prince."

"I'm going to move someplace where no one has ever heard of me and my family," Ivy vowed.

"He's still there with you," Katie said. "That must mean something. However did he find you?"

"I don't know."

Max took the phone from Ivy. "This is Max," he said to her sister. "I knew where your company was located, so I followed her here. Ivy and I ran into each other on the jogging trail. My appearance must have been a shock. She fainted each time she looked at me."

"Ivy did?"

"I take it fainting isn't something she does often?"

He smiled when Ivy groaned and buried her face in her hands. Would this day never be over?

"Of course not," she heard Katie say.

"Why don't you call tomorrow? It's time for her to get ready for bed," Max told her sister.

"Are you staying the night?"

"Of course. She might be ill again."

"Ill?"

"Nauseated. She might need me to hold her head again."

"Oh. Of course."

Ivy reclaimed the phone. "Stop laughing," she demanded of her sister, unable to disguise the prickly tone.

"I'm not," Katie protested. "I'm only smiling."

"And he is not spending the night," Ivy added.

Max indicated he was. "There are too many things to settle between us. Besides, I don't trust you not to take off during the night for parts unknown."

"You are not spending the night," Ivy told him.

"Yes, I am."

"I think I'll let you two argue that out," Katie said. "Call me in the morning, Ivy. You hear?"

"Yes, I hear. Thanks for calling," she said. She hit the off button and placed the phone on the table.

"I am staying." Max crossed his arms over his chest.

"Fine. Stay. See if I care what my neighbors think about some foreigner crashing in my apartment."

"You have plenty of space. There's a guest bedroom. Unless you want me to sleep with you."

She glared at him, aghast that he could even mention such a thing when everything was a mess. Men.

His thick eyebrows rose slightly. "I didn't think so." He gathered up their glasses and the damp napkins under them, then herded her into the house. "Although it's a bit late to be concerned about *that*."

She whirled on him. "If you hadn't…and then you… Anyway, it's all your fault."

Tears pressed close. She would rather die than cry like some spineless wimp in front of him. She fled down the hall and into her room. There she slammed the door and fell across the bed, her hot face pressed desperately into the pillow as she fought for control.

All was quiet in the rest of the house.

After a while—ten minutes or an hour, she had no idea of time—she crept off the bed and into the bathroom. After changing to a nightgown and preparing for bed, she returned and crawled under the sheet.

Fatigue hit her like a sack of rocks, but she couldn't make herself go to sleep. Too many unconnected thoughts drifted in and out of her mind, drawn through the sieve of uncertainty that haunted her.

He'd admitted he'd followed her. But not until almost two months later. He'd waited until she'd known for sure she was expecting. Was it only the baby he was interested in? He hadn't even tried to kiss her good-night or persuade her to share the bed....

With a moan she pulled the pillow over her head.

Chuck was eating on the dining patio of the hotel when Max found him the next morning. "Good. You're here."

His friend smiled over the rim of the coffee cup. "I've been at the hotel all night. Unlike some people."

"Checking on me again?" Max asked, his tone even.

The security advisor shook his head. "Using my deductive skills, I noticed your bed wasn't used last night." Chuck shrugged, then continued. "How's the rose this morning?"

Before Max could answer, the waiter came over with a menu and a glass of water. Max waved the menu aside and ordered coffee. "Black. Strong."

"You need an aspirin?" Chuck asked.

"No. Why?"

"You might when you read this." He held out a couple of sheets of paper. "This came by fax this morning."

Max read over the report from the assistant chief of security. The information recapped an article in a not-too-savory newspaper that covered the northern Mediterranean region. With fair accuracy it detailed his day with Ivy in Lantanya, ending with the sojourn at the resort suite reserved for the royal family. The reporter even knew about the cherries jubilee.

The article then covered the attempted coup and the trial, then Max's departure for Portland to "find the woman who was carrying the future heir to the kingdom."

"How the hell could anyone know this when I didn't until yesterday?" he demanded, tossing the report on the table in disgust.

"A bribe here and there. Interviews with hotel and museum staff. A quick check with an insider at the airlines and a list of foreigners recently entering the country." Chuck studied him for a minute, then added, "The rest is speculation, of course, but it probably didn't take a genius to figure out."

Max heaved an expressive sigh. "My mother was American. She sometimes ranted—in private, naturally—about the lack of privacy royals have. Each time she was pregnant, the press knew it before she did."

"Americans are big on invasion-of-privacy issues," his friend remarked, his manner introspective. "Your mother had three miscarriages before you were born."

"And?"

"The same could happen to the rose. First pregnancies often terminate early. It's as if the body has to get used to the idea first."

Max smiled without humor. "So, should I wait until she comes to term, then bring in the minister after the babe utters its first cry?"

"It's your call, Your Highness."

"I love the way you get out of tight spots by reverting to formality," he said dryly.

Chuck grinned, then became serious again. "How do you feel about Ivy Crosby? Are you willing to spend the rest of your life with her? Your parents were sticklers for honoring their word, including their marriage vows. What if your rose demands the same from you?"

Memories rushed over Max. The brush of a hand over his chest. The sigh of a breath across his lips. The soft touch of those lips against his. The uncertainty, then the hunger. The need. The fulfillment.

"I don't think it would be a hardship."

"Maybe not right now when the blood is hot, but what about later? Marriage lasts a long time, especially with people living to be a hundred nowadays."

"Let's get through the rest of this year before we worry about the next sixty or seventy," Max suggested.

Chuck nodded. "She's smart and dedicated to her work. She's into educational technology systems. She apparently loves children and is concerned for them. That could be a powerful bond, bringing total literacy to Lantanya."

"The educational king and queen." Max smiled. "I like that. She already knows this is part of my plan for the kingdom."

His friend gave him a level look. "But I think you must win her heart as well as her mind for the marriage to be all that's possible."

"I must think of the country first."

"Think of her and a lasting love. Perhaps the rest will follow," Chuck advised solemnly.

Max chuckled. "My security advisor is now my advisor on matters of the heart." He indicated the report lying on the table. "What else is happening in the kingdom by the sea?"

They discussed the functions of the tiny country, including the seized assets of the conspirators. Max was further disappointed upon learning his trusted half uncle had been stealing from the public funds.

When the reports were finished, he sat in silence, his mind going to Ivy and their brief time together. She had come to him so sweetly innocent, trust in her eyes as she'd given herself completely into his hands.

He'd needed that, he realized. Her purity as well as her passion. She was his, by Heaven, and she must come to terms with that. It would soon be time to return home.

"I can give her until the end of the month," he said aloud. "Today is the seventh. By the end of September, we must be wed and on our way home."

"Then you'd better work fast," Chuck told him.

What, Max wondered, would it take to convince Ivy that their futures were as bound together as the roots of the climbing roses that grew so profusely at his island home?

The doorbell rang just as Ivy checked the roasting chicken in the oven. It was golden brown and smelled great. She was also pleased to note that it didn't send her scurrying for the bathroom, hand over mouth.

Glancing at the person outlined against the noon sun, she refused to recognize the disappointment that the silhouette didn't belong to Max.

"Mother, how nice to see you," she said, holding the door wide and leaving it open to the pleasant breeze.

She really was glad to see her mother. There were a hundred things she wanted to ask about babies and such. After all, Sheila had had four children and so should know everything Ivy needed to find out.

"I was at Henri's yesterday and heard several rumors, all of them about you," her mother said, tossing her purse on the entrance hall table, no smile on her face. Due to cosmetic injections, there was no frown, either.

The questions evaporated from Ivy's mind. She assumed a pleasant expression and offered coffee or tea. "Or lunch if you prefer," she said. "It'll be ready soon."

Sheila sniffed delicately. "Roast chicken. It smells quite delicious. You're becoming very domestic, Ivy. Is it because you're pregnant?"

Ivy wasn't surprised at her mother's blunt manner. The older woman had little time to spend on her offspring. "Your hair is lovely," she said instead of answering the question. "That's a new style, isn't it?"

Sheila fluffed the ends of her hair. "Henri said it took ten years off. I think he's right. A person shouldn't get in a rut, I suppose." She eyed Ivy's short curls. "You look like a six-year-old."

It wasn't a compliment. Ivy held back the hot words that rushed to her tongue. Arguing with her mother did little good. Sheila heard only what she wanted.

Now she returned to her original line of thinking. "Are you expecting?"

"It would seem so," Ivy said lightly. She went into the kitchen and prepared two glasses of iced tea, both with lemon, hers with a spoon of sugar, her mother's without. "Shall we sit on the patio?"

Without waiting, she went out the side door and sat at the glass-topped table. When her mother joined her, after making sure the sun wouldn't touch her skin, Ivy slumped into her chair and waited for the lecture.

It occurred to her that instead of enjoying her patio and the new furniture she'd gotten that spring, she mostly sat out there and argued with people, or listened to them tell her what she ought to do. She sipped the tea and waited for the diatribe to begin.

"Whatever were you thinking?" Sheila demanded, taking a seat after making sure the cushions were clean and wouldn't leave marks on her beige silk suit.

"Perhaps I wasn't."

"Don't get smart," her mother warned. "Get rid of it."

Anger, so fierce it was all Ivy could do to control it, rolled over her. "I don't think so. I want the baby."

Sheila studied her for a minute, her eyes narrowed. Ivy could almost hear the wheels turning in her mother's head.

"Whose is it?" Sheila asked.

"No one you know."

"Do you know?" the other woman asked maliciously.

The question lanced into Ivy's heart. That magical night she'd thought she did, but the man she'd so foolishly fallen for hadn't existed. Max Hughes had been part of the dream, not reality.

"Well?" Sheila said.

"Yes, I know."

At that moment, a car stopped at the end of her sidewalk. Ivy recognized Chuck Curland and returned his wave. Max got out and strode up the walk. He spotted her on the patio, waved, then gave her mother a glance, his keen gaze moving from mother to daughter, obviously interested.

Before Ivy could rise, he came in the front entrance and out onto the patio. "Don't get up," he murmured, touching her lightly on the shoulder, leaving a trail of fire along her skin. He smiled at her mother. "I'm Max Hughes. You are Ivy's sister?"

"This is my mother, Sheila Crosby," Ivy said as her mother preened the way she did whenever a handsome man paid her compliments.

He again looked from one to the other. "There is a resemblance. It is easy to see where Ivy got her beauty."

Her mother looked a little startled, as if she'd never considered her daughter's looks a match for her own. She covered it well with a flirty little laugh. "Where did you meet this rogue?" she demanded of Ivy but never took her eyes off Max.

Max sat in the chair beside Ivy, his knee brushing her thigh as he did. "Ivy and I were business acquaintances first, then we became friends."

Although his tone of voice didn't change, Ivy felt a sensual caress in the last word as if he'd stroked her while he spoke. Chill bumps rose on her upper arms.

"Shall I get you a wrap?" he inquired. He rubbed her left arm gently while his eyes delved into hers.

"No. Thanks." Unable to hold that steady gaze, she stared at a slow-moving bee working over a bed of mums along the patio edge.

"The bee hasn't long to store up food for the winter," Max observed. "Nor have we much time."

"Time for what?" Sheila demanded, obviously irritated at being left out of some secret conversation.

Ivy sent Max a pleading glance before watching the bee once more.

"She will have to know," he said, his manner so gentle it brought the sting of tears to her eyes.

"Is he the father?" Sheila blurted out.

Max brought his head up sharply and gave her mother a look that shut her up on the spot. Ivy was amazed. He leaned close, his hair brushing her temple. "We will have to tell her sooner or later."

"I already know about the baby," Sheila informed him waspishly. "So does everyone in town."

He grimaced at Ivy. "I'm sorry that you are being

gossiped about. It was never my intent to embarrass you. Will you forgive me?"

Ivy's throat closed as he lifted her hand to his lips and planted a kiss on each knuckle, then simply held it against his thigh as he observed her.

"There's nothing to forgive," she assured him with fatalistic calm coming over her. "People will gossip no matter what one does."

"True," he agreed. He turned to Sheila. "Ivy and I are expecting a child. In April."

Sheila laid a hand to her chest, each perfectly manicured nail glowing pearl pink against the silk. "Are you also expecting to marry?"

A dangerous glint came into Max's eyes at the sarcastic tone. "Yes," he said, gazing at Ivy.

"No," she corrected.

He stroked her cheek in that endearing way he had that made her want to melt into his arms. "We must, my love."

My love. He'd used that term before. *My love,* he'd murmured to her. Ivy wished he would say it again and that it was true. If she thought he loved her...

"The news of the child has leaked to my country," he continued, now holding her hand pressed to his heart.

"Oh, no," she whispered.

"But yes. My people will expect me to return with my bride and the mother of my child."

"What?" Sheila said.

Max ignored her mother and looked deeply into

Ivy's eyes. "Our son will be heir to the throne," he said softly.

"What?" Sheila gasped, her voice shrill.

"The child might be a girl," Ivy told him.

"It matters not. The firstborn, male or female, inherits the crown."

"Crown? What crown?" Sheila slapped her hand on the table to gain attention.

Neither Ivy nor Max glanced her way. "An illegitimate child inherits nothing," Ivy said.

His hand tightened on hers. "Our child will not be a bastard," he told her in a fierce murmur.

"I think I'm going to faint," her mother said.

Six

Max wanted to tell Sheila to take a hike, but he refrained. She was, after all, mother to Ivy, and would be grandmother to their children. "Please do not faint," he said to her, putting on a teasing smile. "I have enough trouble dealing with your stubborn daughter without taking on more fainting women."

"Well, really," the mother huffed.

"Really," he agreed equably, his gaze never leaving Ivy's set expression. "If you will excuse us, Mrs. Crosby, Ivy and I have matters to discuss and little time to do so."

Ivy looked at him, aghast.

Apparently few people told her mother to get lost, Max realized. He also knew Ivy didn't want to be alone with him. But he would persuade her otherwise. His blood warmed at the thought. He stood and with a gracious manner took Sheila's arm and guided her inside and toward the front door.

"I'm sure you understand," he murmured for her ears alone. "Ivy is shy about her feelings and what happened between us."

"Do you really intend to marry her?" Mrs. Crosby asked, looking somewhat dazed at the idea. "Ivy has no idea of what it takes to be part of a royal family."

Max suppressed irritation. The mother evidently didn't realize how lovely her daughter was or how attractive Ivy's sweet innocence was next to the obvious charms of women such as her. It occurred to him that Sheila was similar in manner to most of the women he'd known all his life, those overconfident of their allure, jaded in their tastes and centered on their own pleasures.

"She is a very special person," he said solemnly. "I think she will make an excellent queen—thoughtful and kind as well as beautiful and intelligent. That is more important than protocol and ritual, which she will easily learn. My people will love her."

There. That should give Sheila something to chew on. He almost chuckled at her slack-jawed expression.

"Well," she said. "How interesting."

"I will call you as soon as things are settled between Ivy and me," he promised. "I hope that soon I will have the honor of calling you Mother Crosby."

He held the door for her, then laughed softly to himself as Sheila obviously didn't know whether to be pleased or furious at his words. She sailed down the sidewalk like a ship in full battle gear and running before the wind.

When he turned, Ivy was standing inside the patio door. "That was a terrible thing to say," she accused. "Now she'll have to have another face-lift or something to get over your referring to her as 'Mother.'"

He laughed again and saw Ivy's mouth compress at the corners. Hunger surged through him. With her curls and baby blue eyes, she looked good enough to eat.

"It was rather funny, though, to see her reaction, don't you think?"

Going to Ivy, he cupped her face in his hands, noting how young and innocent she seemed, not nearly old enough to be the mother of his child. But he was glad she was.

She tried to glare at him, but the gleam in her eyes gave her away. He kissed her nose, then tickled her ribs with one hand while slipping the other behind her head to prevent her from drawing away.

Finally she couldn't hold the merriment in. Her laughter tinkled through the still room like wind chimes playing a fairy song. "You are terrible," she finally scolded, but without heat.

"I know." His voice dropped to a husky depth that he couldn't disguise. "Ivy," he said, an entreaty, did she but know it.

Her eyes widened slightly when she met his gaze. He couldn't suppress the desire that blazed in him or the intensity of the need. Slipping his hand from her side, he touched her hip, then pulled her close.

"Seven weeks without you is a long time," he murmured, wanting her as he'd never wanted another woman. "Too long."

He tasted her lips, her throat while she stood still, trying to resist the pull between them. He could have told her it couldn't be done. The attraction was like gravity, pulling them into each other's orbits like double stars circling each other.

Inhaling sharply as the hunger increased, he was filled with her scent. She smelled of roses that basked in the sun and were kissed by the sea air. A light, fragrant aroma of shampoo and cologne teased his senses and further fanned the flames that were raging deep inside him.

"Ivy," he whispered, urging her closer still, tucking her slender body into his, curves and planes fitting as if made for each other.

"Max…"

Her voice trailed off in uncertainty. He felt her nipples bead against his chest as he rubbed seductively against her, letting her know the strength of his passion and reveling in her response.

"I want you," he said in total honesty. "Now."

Without pausing, he scooped her into his arms and carried her down the short hallway to her room. The bed was neatly made, but, standing her beside him, he quickly took care of that.

"This is not wise," she said.

She tried to speak firmly, but her manner was so hesitant it made his heart somersault. The heat of desire bloomed in her cheeks. He knew her breasts would be flushed, too. "I need to see you. I have to."

Before she could protest, he had the pale-blue knit top slipped over her head and tossed to a nearby chair. Her bra was disposed of as easily. He threw his shirt aside and shucked his slacks and briefs.

"Max," she protested, but softly.

To him, it sounded like a plea, the same as that magical night, a plea for him to come to her.

The buttons of her slacks were no barrier to the rampant urgency that pounded through him. Although she continued murmuring protests, she let him strip those and her lacy briefs from her long, shapely legs.

Once he had them both naked, he again scooped her into his arms and settled on the bed with her in his lap. He piled the pillows against the headboard and half reclined, her body curled against him in a way he found endearing.

"I don't know how I've lived without you the past two months," he told her, planting kisses all over her face, his hands fisted in her springy curls.

"Why didn't you come sooner?"

He took her lips in a long, satisfying kiss before answering. "I wanted to, but there were things I had to take care of. Events unfolded that had to be resolved."

Shaking his head slightly, he fell silent, not willing to discuss betrayal and treason at this moment. He noticed his fingers trembled slightly as he brushed them through her hair. He hadn't felt this young and untried since his first experience with a woman during the freshman year at college.

"You make me feel like a newborn just trying the world on for size." His smile admitted the foolishness of the thought, even though it was true.

Instead of mocking him, she touched his face, then finger combed his hair off his forehead. "Thank you for saying that. Since reading the tabloid, I've wondered about… Well, I wondered if you were acting that night, if it was a pretense. You must have had any number of women who wanted you and would never have refused you."

"There was no one before you," he told her. "No one who counted."

Her eyes darkened, and she looked pensive. "Am I to believe that I count?"

The sadness in her expression hit him square in the chest. "Of course," he chided. "You are the only woman who has conceived my child. I have never allowed that to occur with anyone else."

She pushed herself upright. "We didn't mean for that to happen. It…it was an accident."

Her breasts, with their delicate rosy points, were more than he could resist. "Was it?" he questioned, bending to her and taking one of the rosebuds into his mouth. "Was it?" he asked again, his voice becoming huskier yet.

A tremor rushed through her as he teased her nipple into a tighter bud, first one, then the other. He groaned as hunger played havoc with his control. His body wanted total ravishment without talk or foreplay.

More than that, something in him demanded that he claim her, make her see that she belonged to him and him alone. She'd given her innocence to him that night. Her trust had been a gift he would never forget.

Holding her locked in his embrace, he turned them so he was on top. With lips and hands and body, he stroked her, feeding her desire as well as his own. When she opened her lips to him, when she gasped and clung to him, arms and legs wrapping him in a hot embrace, when she began to move against him, he was elated.

"Now," he murmured, finding her ready.

Rising on one arm, aware of her gaze, he entered her, merging them with nothing between them but the need they shared.

He kissed her a thousand times and caressed her to his heart's desire. She returned each caress, each kiss, until his senses were filled with her. Only her. When she cried out, he closed his eyes and held on, giving her every bit of pleasure that he could.

Her demands incited him past control as she writhed under him like a dancing flame. An incandescent glow filled his soul.

Together they sought the intense rhythm of release. Together they reached the bliss, her throaty cries a counterpoint to the deep groan of total satisfaction he found in her arms.

Seconds, minutes, eons passed while their breathing slowed to normal. He rested beside her, their bodies still intimately joined. Odd, but he didn't want to lose the connection with her, as if, in doing so, he might lose her.

Which was likely true.

They connected completely this way, but when the passion was spent, reason would intercede, making her wary of him as a man and possible lifetime mate. He would show her—

From the kitchen came the sound of a timer. He raised his head and looked at her to see if she knew what it was.

"Lunch is ready," she said.

The statement seemed so ordinary and so very, very right that he laughed, causing them to separate. He cupped her face and kissed her rosy lips. "Shall we eat, then? I admit I'm hungry for food now that the other, more demanding hunger is satisfied."

She wouldn't meet his eyes. "We shouldn't—"

He laid a finger over her mouth. "It was the best thing I've ever known. I don't regret it, not now nor in the past when we shared the same magic moments."

"If we hadn't met, if this—" she gestured toward her abdomen to indicate the pregnancy "—hadn't happened, where would you have looked for a bride?"

"It did happen, so we don't have to consider that." He smiled to reassure her. "My security advisor assures me that an American heiress is quite acceptable."

"We don't know each other."

"Don't we?" he demanded, impatient with her qualms. "I think we knew each other very well."

"That was physical."

"The physical union of a man and woman is one of the foundations the world is built on."

Ivy knew there must be one final argument, one supreme bit of logic she could employ that would refute for all time his determination on marriage. Before the thought had hardly formed, she knew she didn't want to find such an argument.

Despair gripped her. "I don't know *you*, Your Highness. The man I met in Lantanya was Max Hughes, businessman. With that man, I found a thousand things we shared in common. What do I share with a king?"

His eyes roamed over her, making her aware of her nakedness. She felt so exposed, in more ways than one, as he considered her question. She saw his chest rise, then fall as he expelled a heavy breath.

Sitting on the side of the bed, he took her hands. "Even a king must be allowed his private moments. At those times he is only a man with a man's needs and desires, with a man's longing for a retreat from the world and its problems. For me, you are that retreat."

His smile was solemn as she searched his face for the meaning behind the words. Was he sincere, or was this a ruse to get his way? He was a man of the world. He would have learned long ago the right words to use to bend another to his will.

"You want the child," she began.

"Yes," he said adamantly.

"And I come as part of the package."

"A very lovely package." He laid the tips of his fingers against her temples. "You Americans. You analyze everything to death. Can't you see that some things are meant to be?"

She shook her head.

"Stubborn," he murmured, then continued. "The fate that brought us together and gave us that one sweet night as lovers was predestined. It was written in the stars. We as humans need only accept what the gods have decreed."

Ivy wanted to believe him, but a lifetime of caution, of observing what people do, not what they say, made it too difficult to believe in kismet and fate and predestination.

"Perhaps, like Romeo and Juliet, it was a time that was never meant to be," she told him.

The timer dinged again.

Rolling to the far side of the bed, she rose and rushed into the bathroom, closing the door to signify her wish to be alone, although she didn't lock it. After showering, she realized she'd forgotten clothing.

Wrapping the towel around her, she opened the door and peered out. The room was empty.

Going to the closet, she selected loose dark-beige slacks with a drawstring waist and a gold top with beige piping around the scoop neckline and raglan sleeves. She put on sunscreen, light makeup and coral lipstick. With brown loafers on her feet and gold hoops in her ears, she was ready to face the world.

Well, this little corner of it at any rate, she corrected, hearing Max in the kitchen. Her heart went into a swan dive before she could order it to straighten up.

His back was to her when she entered the room.

His hair was damp, so he must have used the guest bath to shower. She watched him set the table, as competent at that as he was at everything else. Including making love.

No! She mustn't think about that.

The roasted chicken and the vegetables she'd cooked with it were on a platter in the center of the pale blue tablecloth he'd found in the sideboard. After folding two matching napkins so that they resembled flowers, he placed them in fluted champagne glasses by each plate.

When he turned toward the kitchen, he saw her. His perfect smile appeared, a homing device for her heart like the beam of a lighthouse guiding a lost ship to safety. Longing rose in her. She wanted to go to him and rest in his arms and let him take care of her and the future.

He placed a hand on his chest and stared at her as if under an enchantment. When he spoke, his voice was soft, deep, beguiling.

"Be still, my heart, 'tis naught
But a vision, an earthly delight wrought
From the yearnings of a soul stricken
By loneliness of a most dismal sort."

Ivy swallowed as emotion rose to her throat. "Very affecting," she mocked gently because the words had moved her. "Did you make it up?"

He shook his head. "An obscure Lantanyan poet, lovesick for a woman denied to him."

"Why? What happened? Did her parents refuse to let her marry him?"

"No. She was already married."

"Oh."

"To my father," he finished. He pulled out a chair and gestured for her to be seated. With an elegant flourish, he snapped open the napkin and laid it across her lap. His hand touched her shoulder and lingered a second before he brought tall glasses of iced tea to the table and joined her.

"Did she love the poet?" Ivy asked, unable to contain her curiosity about his family.

Max laid his napkin in his lap, then gazed at Ivy as if weighing the answer. "As a friend," he said. "My mother would never have allowed an inappropriate emotion to intrude between her and my father."

Ivy mulled this over. "It was a love match? Your parents were in love?"

"They were devoted to each other."

She wasn't sure that answered her question. "Are love and devotion the same?"

Max looked up from buttering a roll. He spoke with great assurance, as if he knew exactly what he was talking about. "For a king and queen, yes. They were dedicated to each other, to their family and to the country. Together they worked toward a common goal for the good of all."

"They shared a vision," Ivy concluded, but still, that wasn't the question. "But is that love?"

Max laid the knife across the edge of the bread plate and studied her. "It was enough to sustain them through forty-four years of marriage. What is it you want to know?"

"Were they faithful to each other?" she asked bluntly.

His handsome, somewhat arrogant face relaxed. "Ah, that is what bothers you," he said gently. "Yes, they were faithful as far as I know. There were never any rumors about either of them, although the tabloids seized upon the slightest pretext to paint a different picture. That is something you will have to resign yourself to. As my queen, you will have your every word, every gesture interpreted in the worst possible manner."

"Life in the public eye," she murmured.

"Yes. But there will be private moments, ones we will share with no one but each other. Other times will be enjoyed with our children and friends. Those are the moments we will cherish and remember when the paparazzi print their lies and innuendoes about our lives."

"I'm afraid of the lies," she said quietly. "How does one separate them from the truth?"

Reaching across the table, he tilted her chin so he could gaze into her eyes. "I have no doubts about your loyalty," he said. "So the question in your mind is about mine." He paused, then said, "My word of honor, I will be faithful to my American rose."

She hadn't expected the pledge or the intensity in his voice as he spoke. The words blew through her like a gale, forcing her to hold her doubts up to a careful scrutiny in the face of his surety. Scenes from her stormy childhood darted through her inner vision.

"My parents—"

"We are not them," Max interrupted before she could tell him about their turbulent marriage. "We are shaped by our past to a certain extent, but we have choices. We can follow a road of our own choosing."

"How do we know which one is best?"

His sudden smile was teasing, but totally confident. "Let the stars be your guide."

She gave him a severe frown. "First you say we do the choosing, then you advise letting fate or whatever make the choices for us. That makes no sense."

"It does," he said softly. "You spent a night in my arms. Was that fate or our own choice in answering the irresistible attraction between us? A child came of that night. We didn't plan that, but it happened. Fate? Or a willing risk on our part?"

No answer came to her.

"Well?" he demanded.

"I don't know," she said defiantly.

"In either case, the results are the same."

The baby. She laid a hand on her abdomen, feeling a whiplash of emotion too strong to be denied. She wanted the child. Already the bonds of love formed a protective casing around the tiny life that bloomed inside her.

"I want the child," she told him.

His nod indicated he had never thought otherwise. "So do I. Did you think I wouldn't?"

"I didn't know. The man I thought was the father turned out to be someone else."

They were silent for the remainder of the meal. Max's gaze was moody as he stared out the patio door. Ivy put the leftovers away and placed the used dishes in the dishwasher. When there was nothing left to do, she refilled their tea glasses and indicated she was going outside.

On the patio, she smiled and waved to the golfers who were searching the creek area for a lost ball, the same two men who'd nearly beaned her the other day.

Friday. Two days ago. And she'd already succumbed—again!—to the passion that boiled between her and Max at the slightest glance. What had happened to her common sense?

"Don't beat it to death," he advised, joining her. He, too, waved at the men.

"You know what I find odd?" she said after a moment.

"What?"

"From what I've read, royalty has had illegitimate children throughout history without a thought to their well-being or to their gaining the throne, so why are you concerned?"

A large, masculine hand closed over hers. His grip didn't hurt, but she was immediately aware of the power there, and the fact that he was furious with her.

"I care about the child," he said in a low, dangerous tone. "It is my flesh and blood as well as yours. Don't ever question my motives about it again. Do you hear?"

She nodded slowly, her heart pounding a dull thud of fear throughout her body.

He removed his hand from hers. His face seemed cast in stone as he said, "You're afraid of me. You've shared total physical intimacy with me, yet you're afraid."

"Not of you."

"Then what?"

"Of the marriage. I can't see that it has a chance of success. Our lives are so different."

"My father married an American. Their marriage worked."

She wondered if it really did, or if it was a facade they presented to the world. Looking at Max, she realized he was convinced. As a child in the home, he would have known of any discord. Children always did. "Your family life was different from mine. My parents divorced soon after I was born. Neither tragedy nor a new baby kept them together."

Falling silent, she studied him while his gaze roamed restlessly over the pleasant pastoral scene. A slight frown indented a line over the bridge of his nose.

"I can offer you and the child a good home and all the advantages of wealth and education the world offers," he told her. "Think of it as a business merger, if you will. There is one stipulation. There can be no divorce."

Ivy found herself again trembling next to an abyss. On this side, she was safe but alone. On the other, she would have marriage, companionship and a family—things she ardently wanted—but they came at great risk and a high price. If the marriage failed, she would be trapped.

But then, so would he.

"If the marriage is a mistake," she began.

"Then we will suffer, but we will also bear it," he said, finishing the thought for her. A smile slowly curved across his mouth. "Or it may be bliss. We've already had some samples of that."

Oh, yes, she knew about the bliss. In his arms she couldn't think. He incited feelings she'd never known existed. Unfortunately, they couldn't stay in bed all the time. A sigh worked its way out of her. "I don't think passion lasts. It never seemed to for my mother and father."

"I don't know about your father, but your mother is not a good example, if you will forgive me for saying so."

"True."

"I understand your childhood experiences have left you wary, but you must put that behind you now and think of the future." He shifted closer and laid his hand over her abdomen. "We can't ignore the result of our passion, and there's no need to," he said with great practicality. "We are a match in many ways. The marriage will be good."

Looking into his eyes and the certainty she witnessed there, she wanted to believe him.

Truly she wanted to…

Seven

Monday morning came too early for Ivy. Max had left her apartment last night when she'd indicated she was going to bed. Alone. He'd grinned, kissed her and left, making sure she locked the door behind him.

She dressed for work in black slacks and a white-and-black knit top. Her black tasseled loafers were comfortable, a part of her "uniform" for the office. After drying her hair and brushing it as smooth as it would go, she tied a black scarf around her head to tame the curls and to make her look older.

As part of her healthier life-style, she prepared oatmeal in the microwave and ate it with whole wheat toast. She found it did wonders for calming her unreliable tummy.

In fact, she felt quite fit by the time she arrived at

the headquarters of Crosby Systems and parked at the far corner of the parking lot so she'd have to walk a good distance to her office. Once in the office, she saw the department secretary had set up the meeting Ivy had requested for nine that morning. It was now eight-thirty.

After going over memos, e-mails and regular mail, she got a cup of coffee and headed for the conference room next door. No one else had arrived yet. She laid out the plans she and her team had worked on. It was now in the final stages and, if approved by Lantanya's ministry of education, would go into production.

That would necessitate her staying in Lantanya for weeks while the plan was implemented to oversee it and make sure it was installed according to the specifications.

Hearing voices in the hall, she took her seat at the head of the table and pushed a button for a projection screen to lower at the other end of the room. The three systems engineers assigned to her project filed in.

She noticed they were unusually quiet. Then she understood why.

Her brother entered the room and with him, wearing a guest badge, was Max.

Trent's eyes met hers. He smiled slightly. "We have a guest," he said, his gaze taking in the whole team. "Max Hughes is a consultant for Lantanya. He wants to go over the plans before they are sent to the officials for final approval. I believe you know him, Ivy, so I'll leave you to introduce the others."

"All right," she heard herself say. Her voice, to her ears, sounded as if she spoke from a deep well.

"Come to my office about a quarter to twelve," Trent told her. "We'll go to lunch at the country club. Father and Toni will join us."

Ivy nodded.

Trent left them, closing the door as he did. Ivy glanced at one of the engineers. At her unspoken request, he rose from the chair on her right and went to another.

"Please join us," she said to Max.

"Thank you." Max smiled at the group. "I'm pleased to be able to take part at this stage of the planning."

Ivy introduced each of the men and outlined their part in the system plans. "I have the flow charts back from drafting, so we can begin," she finished, and dimmed the lights so they could easily see the screen.

Onto the projector she laid the first sheet, which was covered with the "big picture" diagrams for a cable system with computers and filters at each school in Lantanya.

"The signals will be digital and come from a commercial satellite network," she explained to Max. "Digital is faster than the analog system you are using at present at the university level. Those will be replaced."

Max nodded. "Could we incorporate a training program so that graduate students would do the actual installations and setup of the computers and software?"

"That would slow us down," her chief engineer said, his frown indicating he didn't care for the idea.

"But it can be done," Ivy interrupted. "Your graduate systems engineers can handle the computer-modem setup at each location under our senior engineer. We've already agreed to use local labor for installing the cables and related equipment."

"Perfect," Max murmured. "Please continue."

Ivy led the discussion on the final components of the system as the team went over the plans down to the final detail. They found no mistakes on the drawings and made only one minor modification to the overall system.

Max occasionally asked a question, but otherwise listened attentively. After her initial tension dissipated, Ivy became engrossed in the work, although she never lost her awareness of the man who sat on her right, his dark eyes alert and taking in everything.

They stopped for a short break at ten-thirty, then finished up the meeting at eleven-thirty. Ivy thanked them for their hard work on the project, handed the flow chart sheets to the head engineer and turned off the projector.

"Shall we see if Trent is ready?" she asked Max, pausing at the light switch. When he nodded, she flicked out the light and led the way to her brother's office. She was acutely aware of Max's hand on the small of her back, big and warm and confident, as they walked down the hall.

Trent was on the phone, but his secretary told

them to go on in. He smiled and waved them to a seat while he finished the conversation.

Ivy, listening, realized one of their employees had been injured on the job. Her brother was talking to the doctor on the case.

"Crosby Systems will pick up the tab, no matter what the insurance company does," Trent said firmly, "so start the physical therapy when he's ready."

Ivy was proud of Trent. At thirty-seven, he was CEO of the firm and very good at his job. Their father had trained him to be. Like Jack Crosby, Trent was a workaholic and he also was divorced. Ivy had been amazed when Trent had married a woman so like their mother in character that it was scary.

Vain and self-centered, his wife had been a model. Her life had revolved around her beauty and social engagements, leaving little time for Trent and the family he'd wanted. Thank goodness there had been no children.

Katie and Trent were fairly close, due to working together for years, and Katie had told her all about their big brother's disastrous marriage.

Ivy stole a glance at Max. Marriage was so uncertain, even when the couple shared the same background. Passion didn't seem to be a very reliable criterion.

"Ready?" Trent asked. "Dad and Toni are holding a table for us."

The three of them went together in Trent's car. Ten minutes later they arrived and parked in the shade of an old oak tree near the entrance to the club. Ivy realized she'd forgotten to prepare Max for her father and his wife.

"Hello. I see you finally got here," Jack Crosby said, standing when he saw them.

Ivy placed a duty kiss on his cheek, then stood aside while he spoke to Trent and shook hands with Max when her brother introduced the men. Ivy let her father introduce his second wife, Toni.

Max took the woman's hand and gave an elegant little bow. His only expression was a pleasant smile. No surprise showed in his eyes as it did in most people's upon meeting the stepmother, who was thirty-seven to Jack Crosby's sixty-nine years. Thirty-two years' difference.

But recalling what she'd read about other marriages among royalty, a large age difference didn't seem to bother them as long as the woman produced the necessary heir. And maybe a spare.

Ivy was jolted by how cynical she sounded, even to herself.

As the group was seated, she had to admit Toni wasn't the usual trophy wife. She held an MBA from a prestigious school back east. After she was hired for a position in the marketing department, Jack had made her his executive assistant before he'd married her and retired.

Actually Toni had been an asset to Jack and to the company. She was still his confidante and trustworthy advisor. She and Katie got along well, too. Not that Ivy had any quarrel with her stepmother, but they weren't close.

"You look familiar," Toni now said, tilting her head and studying Max. "Your accent is slight but detectable. European. Italian, perhaps?"

"You have an excellent ear. I'm from Lantanya, just off the coast of Italy," Max told her. "An island kingdom few people remember exists."

"Trent tells me you're a consultant to the education minister there," Jack said, a question in his voice.

Ivy was aware of Max's slight hesitation and his glance at her before he replied, "In a manner of speaking."

Apparently Katie hadn't told Trent of Max's real identity. She didn't know whether this was the time to do so or not. The moment passed before she reached a decision as the waiter brought the day's specials to their attention.

"I think I'll have the salmon," Toni said. "You should, too, darling," she said to her husband. "It's supposed to be good for the heart."

"Yes, dear," her father said meekly, then laughed as his wife balled her fist and tapped him on the shoulder.

Ivy smiled at their playfulness. She'd always assumed Toni had married Jack for his money and position, but after the woman's concern at his last heart attack, which was the second one in five years, Ivy wasn't so sure.

Maybe Toni did love Jack…or at least was smart enough to keep up the pretense that she did. Dear ol' Dad had been a womanizer all his life. It would take a sharp gal to keep his attention. Toni, with her intelligence and blond-haired, blue-eyed, model-perfect looks, seemed able to do that.

But Ivy didn't envy her stepmother the job. It wasn't the life she wanted with her mate, always having to strive to keep his interest, never letting your guard down and staying on the lookout for other women wanting your position. She wanted a husband she could trust.

Mentally sighing, she studied Max as he chatted with the others, completely at ease in this environment. She could imagine their life together during their private moments, those in which they indulged the wild passion between them, but she feared privacy would be a rare thing in their lives.

What if Max went to other women when she wasn't available, just as her father had done to her mother?

The idea caused her such pain that she couldn't think about it with others around. It brought her too low, too close to the brink of tears.

"Ivy," Max said gently.

She blinked, realized she was still staring and looked away from his handsome face.

"Your order?" he coaxed.

"Oh. Uh, I'll have the salmon, too." She hadn't heard her father order it, but she assumed he had. "No potatoes. A double serving of the mixed veggies, please."

After Max and Trent put in their order, the waiter left. Ivy tried to keep her mind on the discussion of the weather and her father's golf score.

For his age, he looked really good, Ivy mused. His blond hair, once very much like hers, had gone white. He had a golfer's tan and kept his weight in check. Having come from a poor family, he was proud of starting his own company and making millions, and looked the part.

"He'd better watch his game," Toni declared. "I'm very close to beating him." She tossed her head and gave Jack a challenging oblique glance, definitely flirty.

Maybe that was the way to keep a man's attention. Flirt with him, throw challenges at him, keep him guessing about one's motives, the hidden messages behind the teasing tone.

Ivy sighed. She didn't think she was cut out for that kind of intrigue and double-entendre teasing.

Max leaned close. "Stop worrying," he said sternly.

"I can't," she admitted.

"You're not in this alone, you know."

She gazed into his eyes, which seemed so deep that she could see right into his soul. For a long minute he left himself open to her, then he smiled and took her hand under cover of the table.

"Let me do the worrying," he murmured. "Let's tell your father we plan to marry before the end of the month."

A horrible sense of disaster rolled over her, leaving her speechless.

"I can see the idea appeals to you," he said with a sardonic twist and a flicker of other emotions in his eyes that she couldn't read.

Ivy had to open her mouth and force herself to breathe. It was then that she noticed her relatives were staring at her and Max. She tried to smile, but her lips trembled too much, and she gave up the effort.

Max had no such trouble. "As you may have guessed," he said in a lazy drawl, "I'm courting Ivy. Or trying to. She's stubborn, as I'm sure you've realized."

Ivy wanted to sink right through the floor as four pairs of eyes observed her with differing expressions. She decided she would kill Max as soon as they were alone.

Max smiled to himself as he rode home with Ivy at five-thirty that afternoon. She was furious with him for telling her family he was courting her. She was also trying not to show it. He theorized she didn't want to give him the satisfaction of knowing he got to her.

He wanted to do just that, in more ways than one.

The blood surged hotly through his body. Being with her all day had fueled his ardor instead of cooling it. Had she but known it, her refusal to bend to his wishes only made the challenge that much more interesting.

"Out with it before you explode," he told her when she pulled onto the freeway.

She shot him a searing glance. "Why did you tell my family that we—that you—that—"

"I'm courting you? I am."

"Don't be ridiculous."

"It's the only solution," he told her. "I know you don't think we know each other well enough for marriage, so I'm giving you the time you need. We'll do the things other couples do while dating."

"Huh. Where do you want me to drop you?" she asked, icicles coating the words.

"Wherever you're going is fine."

"I'm going home."

"That's where I'm going, too."

"You're not coming home with me."

"I thought we would have dinner and enjoy a quiet evening together. It's something I rarely get to do."

"Poor overworked prince," she scoffed.

He fingered one of her riotous curls, then leaned close. "We could talk, have dinner, talk, make love, then talk some more."

"Don't," she said on a ragged breath.

"Sorry. I didn't mean to upset you. It's just that I like teasing you. Even a prince needs someone to share a lighter moment with. There could be other moments, too," he said huskily, thinking of all the things they could do.

When her nipples contracted and stood out against the soft knit top, he had to swallow hard and think of icy mountain streams. Not that it did any good.

He gently cupped the alluring mound. "You respond so naturally. Your body knows what it wants," he said. "I love the way your breasts flush with desire, the tips as pink and firm as miniature rosebuds.

I like to run my tongue over them and feel their hardness. I like to hear you gasp my name and feel your hands on me, urging me closer."

Twin flags of color flew to her cheeks. He brushed the back of a finger over the smooth, flushed skin.

"I like the satin softness of you, the slick dew of passion that draws me like a bee to nectar when you're ready for me."

"Please," she whispered.

He inhaled deeply, let it out heavily, but, granting mercy on both of them, settled against the seat as she turned onto the exit ramp at her apartment complex.

When she'd come to a complete stop in her parking space and turned off the engine, she faced him. "This is a game to you. You're the hunter. I'm the prey."

"The chase is fun," he admitted, then regretted the words when something akin to pain flashed through her eyes. The rose took love and marriage and family very seriously. For that matter, so did he. He had to make her see that.

When she got out of the vehicle, he followed suit and went with her up the sidewalk with its attractive border of flowers. He took her hand and was gratified when she didn't pull away.

"But life is more than that," he continued. "Some people waste their time dashing from one romance to another. They don't stick it out through the hard times, and they never know the pride and contentment of building a life with one person over the long haul."

She stopped at the door, key in hand, and studied him as if trying to discover what made him tick. He held still and let her look. She was the only person he'd ever let himself be vulnerable to—a difficult thing to do.

Shaking her head slightly, she turned back to the door. When she inserted the key into the bolt, the door swung open on its own.

"Stay put," he ordered, pushing Ivy behind him.

Kicking the door open with his foot, he surveyed the living room and kitchen. Going inside, he peered behind the sofa, checked the draperies and the shadows behind a potted plant, then went into the kitchen.

"What is it?" she asked, right behind him. "Do you think someone broke in?"

"Yes, I think someone broke in," he told her, his jaw muscles stiff with worry. "Don't you ever do as you're told?"

"Not often," she admitted, going to the pantry and opening the door. "There's no one in here."

He controlled his exasperation with effort and knew a moment of sympathy for Chuck in trying to guard him when he was being pigheaded. "Let's check the bedrooms. Do you want to go first or shall I?"

"You." She managed to look contrite.

Leading the way, he checked the apartment thoroughly, Ivy on his heels the entire time. The place was vacant.

"Empty," he said, satisfied this was true.

"But someone has been here," she told him, folding her arms over her waist. "I feel a sense of violation." Her laughter was feeble. "Probably overreaction."

"Maybe not. Chuck believes in gut instinct. He thinks you subconsciously pick up clues that don't immediately make an impact on your mind. A faint trace of another's scent, something moved an inch to the side, that sort of thing."

"Should we call the police?"

Max made a decision and shook his head. "I'll call Chuck. He's the best investigator I know."

An hour later the security advisor laid two tiny devices on the dining room table where Max and Ivy waited while he checked out the apartment. "The place has been bugged, I'm afraid."

"Who?" Ivy questioned, puzzlement in her eyes. "Why?"

"That's what we need to find out," Chuck told them. "Is it because of Max? Or you?"

"Why would anyone be interested in me?" she asked, then glanced at Max.

Chuck answered. "Because of Crosby Systems. Competition is fierce in the computer industry. Your company is involved in several lucrative contracts. *You* are heading up a multimillion-dollar project. If an enemy could find a way to discredit you, that might bring the whole enterprise into question or cause a government investigation."

"Especially if it was whispered in the right ears that the project involves sensitive technology," Max added. "That could stop everything in its tracks."

"The project was approved by the State Department," Ivy told the two men. "It was all cleared before we did the detail planning."

"All's fair in politics and international intrigue," Chuck said with a shrug.

Max observed as Ivy absorbed this information. When her eyes darted to him, he held her gaze. *Yes, this is what my life is like,* he silently told her. *Yes, you would be part of the rumors and intrigues as my wife.*

When she looked away, he rose and paced restlessly to the patio door. Gazing at the lovely September landscape, he wished he were free to love as he pleased without giving a thought to kingdoms and international relationships.

With a sigh, he turned toward the room once more. Even a small country such as his was a player on the world stage. His queen would have to learn to live with that.

Heaviness descended on his spirits. His internal landscape darkened, like a night without even the moon's pale gleam to brighten his way.

"What now?" Chuck asked, looking at him.

"We can't leave Ivy here alone."

His security chief nodded. "Do we stay here or take her to the hotel? The latter would be the best, I think."

Ivy held up a hand to stop the discussion. "Wait a minute. I'm not going anywhere."

Max glanced at Chuck and shrugged. "Okay. We'll stay here." He gave her a hard look. "Either way, there'll be no arguing."

She didn't back down. "What do you think is going to happen to me? No one would dare hurt Jack Crosby's kid."

"Years ago someone kidnapped one of the Logan boys. He was playing with your brother at the time," Chuck reminded her. He turned to Max. "We'd better tell her what happened in Lantanya the past few weeks."

"There was a trial for treason," she said. "It was on the news one night. I guess they couldn't get any experts to talk about it because it never came up again."

Max nodded. "I had to sentence my uncle and one of our ministers to prison."

A stricken expression came into her lovely eyes. "That's what you were doing before coming here?"

"Before coming for you," he said softly. "Yes."

"They tried to kill you."

He lifted a hand to caress her cheek and allay her fears. "You saved my life. I was with you the night the attempt was made."

"How horrible," she whispered.

He smiled, although it was with sadness. "No, that part was good. It was the trial and sentencing that was horrible. I'd trusted those men, you see."

Tears brimmed on her lashes. The pain she felt was for him, he realized. He pulled her to his chest and felt the hot tears soak through his shirt.

"I'll, uh, leave you two to, uh, discuss things," Chuck said, moving toward the door. "I don't think there's any immediate danger, but you should come to the hotel to spend the night."

"We will," Max assured him.

Chuck exited, closing the door and making sure it locked. Ivy tilted her head back and stared at him with her tear-washed eyes.

"I couldn't bear it if you died."

Max couldn't bear her grief. He caught her face between his hands and kissed her hotly, urgently. "Come with me," he said. "I won't be able to rest until you do."

"To the hotel?" she asked.

He hesitated, then nodded. "For now." Before she could speak, he added, "We'll decide other things at other times. Get what you need, and let's go."

"I can go to my sister's place. Or my father's."

"I need you with me."

To his surprised relief, she didn't argue, but packed a bag and handed him the keys to her car when she was ready. Something turned over in his heart, demanding attention, but there was no time at the present.

At the hotel he whisked Ivy to the top floor and the corner suite he and Chuck shared. A large living area, complete with a kitchen and dining table, separated the two bedrooms. Max had the one with king-size bed.

He carried Ivy's luggage to his room. "You'll sleep in here."

"Where will you sleep?" she asked.

"Chuck has two beds in his room. The sofa makes a bed, too, I think." He gave her a deliberately lascivious stare meant to dispel the worry in her face. "Or I can sleep in here with you."

He found himself waiting anxiously for her next words.

"Men," she scoffed and rolled her eyes. The worry was still there, but so was a smile. "You may as well stay here, too. Otherwise, I'd never get any sleep for worrying."

Max caught her to him. He had to control his strength in order not to hold her too tightly. He didn't want to leave bruises on her fair skin.

"Thanks," he said lightly, although he couldn't stop his voice dropping to a husky note as hunger shot through him like a blaze from a flame thrower. He cupped her face and placed a kiss on the tip of her nose. "You just want to be in the thick of things," he accused.

She gazed up at him, her manner earnest, her honesty so tangible he could feel it surrounding her like a force field. When she laid both hands on his chest—not to hold him off, but because she wanted to touch him, he realized—it did things to his insides.

"My lovely, compassionate princess," he whispered. "It would be so easy to take advantage of your tender heart."

She shook her head in brief denial, then took a deep breath that caused her breasts to brush his chest. "I will marry you," she said, looking him in the eye. "On one condition."

For a moment he couldn't believe he was hearing correctly, but her steadfast gaze told him she was serious. "What is the condition?"

"You told my family you were courting me…."

When her voice trailed off, he nodded to encourage her to go on.

She swallowed, then said, "I want you to do that. Court me. And mean it."

"I do mean it," he told her, somewhat puzzled. "What are you asking?"

"I want you to court me as if…as if we were madly in love."

It would be very easy to murmur the words. He had only to open his mouth and say the three words she wanted from him and she would accept him. But she was too fine, too honorable for him to treat her needs cavalierly.

"I have feelings for you." That much was very true.

"But not love," she concluded.

"Foul deeds have been excused in the name of love. I have heard people declare love, then stab the supposed loved one in the back. It is a word that is much used and little honored, I'm afraid."

Her gaze flickered down, then back to his. A veil had been drawn across her emotions. "I see," she said quietly.

It hurt him someplace deep inside to see that shield erected between them. "Love has not served me well of late," he tried to explain. "My father's half brother, a man I trusted and, with a child's faith, assumed would never betray me, did just that—"

"He arranged the assassination attempt the night you stayed with me?" she interrupted, looking so fierce on his behalf he wanted to kiss her until they were both senseless.

Holding the swirl of emotions in check, he nodded. "Yes. So I find I'm somewhat skeptical about declarations of devotion at the moment. Words are cheap. It is action that speaks of the intent of the heart. I asked you to be my wife and my queen. It is something I've never done."

"Because of the child."

"That and other things." He gazed into her eyes. "We are physically attracted to each other. I admire you for your intelligence and for your integrity. More than all those, though, I like you as a person. I like being with you even without making love. Even when we quarrel."

He couldn't help but grin as she obviously tried to sort through all this and decide if he was telling the truth. He laughed when she frowned in exasperation.

"I will court you, my lovely, delicate rose," he whispered, leaning close so that he smelled the sweet scent of her. "And it will be done with honesty and sincerity. If you consent to marriage, upon my honor, I will respect our vows. All of them."

There. He had made his pledge. It was up to her whether she would accept his word.

Her sudden smile dazzled him. Raising both hands to his face, she held him gently and said, "Then let the courtship begin."

Her kiss surprised and pleased him. For ten seconds he tried to keep it light, but that was as long as his control lasted. He wrapped her in his arms until he could feel every curve of her luscious body.

She broke the kiss. "A courtship," she said with ragged determination, "must be platonic. If we make love, it will confuse things."

He groaned, then valiantly released her and wondered if she knew what she was asking. A platonic courtship? He doubted he would live through it.

Eight

Ivy woke with a jerk. She was disoriented, but it took only a glance at the luxurious suite to remind her where she was. Max was nowhere in sight. After checking all exits last night as if he were doing a crime scene investigation, he'd left her and slept on the bed hidden in a cherry armoire in the elegant living room.

After a moment's thought, she recalled it was Tuesday and a workday. It was hard for her to believe it had been a mere week since she'd bought the pregnancy test kit and the tabloid that had identified the father of her child.

She felt she'd lived several lifetimes in seven days. In some ways she had. First there'd been the pregnancy test, then a lover who'd turned into a prince—but not due to her magical kiss.

Ha. She mocked the turbulent feelings this thought evoked.

And finally there had been the meeting on the jogging trail and the dramatic faint.

She groaned, then rose carefully, mindful of the unpredictability of her tummy these days. She showered and dressed, ran the stream of hot air from the blow dryer over her hair for two minutes, then went into the other room.

No one was there. A note from Max told her he and Chuck were out jogging. He'd ordered breakfast to be brought to the suite at eight. She checked the clock on the wall in the tiny kitchen. Fifteen minutes before the hour.

Spotting the coffeemaker, she put on a pot to brew and nibbled on a package of peanut butter crackers she found in a cabinet. That got her through the queasy part of the day. By the time the coffee was done, she felt ready to face any problem.

Until Max walked in the door.

The freshness of the day seemed to cling to his muscular form as he entered. He saw her and headed toward the counter that separated the kitchen from the large living and dining area. His jogging clothes were soaked with perspiration, and the heated scent of his body enfolded her in warmth and a trill of excitement.

She couldn't help but look him over. He exuded all the alluring assets of the alpha male. He was virile, confident and courageous. His shoulders were broad, his chest deep, his arms and legs laced with muscles. Handsome. Powerful. A leader among men. Literally.

At the counter, he leaned forward, took her cup and stole a sip, then kissed her with such tender passion, it drove the breath right from her body.

"I missed you last night," he murmured, handing the cup back and letting his gaze drift over her face, skim her breasts that jutted wantonly against her white sweater, and finally sweep down her blue slacks to her loafers before returning to rest on her abdomen. "How are you feeling?"

"Fine."

"No nausea?"

"No." She refused to blush at the intimate questions.

"Breakfast should be here soon. I'll be back." He headed for his room and closed the door behind him.

Feeling weak and foolish, she topped up the coffee and took a seat in a comfortable club chair. She'd hardly gotten settled when the doorbell rang.

"Keep your seat," Chuck advised, coming out of the other bedroom that was part of the suite. He opened the door and greeted the room service waiter.

Chuck was freshly showered, Ivy noted, and dressed in dark slacks, a white shirt and a tie. He directed the waiter to place the food on the gleaming cherry dining table, his manner almost brusque. The waiter got busy, and by the time he exited, Max returned.

"Did I hear someone say food?" he asked, striding across the room as if he commanded the world.

His smile was dazzling when he offered her his arm and escorted her to the table. He seated her to his right while Chuck took the chair to the left of the head of the table.

"I've spoken with your brother," Max told her.

"Trent? Why?"

"Because you may be in danger. He agrees that you should stay under my watchful eye while Chuck and your company's security agents check out your place."

"Check it for what?" She was beginning to feel she was playing a scene in a B-rated movie and her lines were the worst ones.

"Fingerprints. He thinks we should notify the FBI."

"I agree," Chuck said. "They need to know what's at stake here."

"What?" Ivy asked. "What's at stake?"

Those thick, black eyebrows that she loved to stroke rose slightly in patient irony. "I think he's referring to us and the child."

"To your life," Chuck stated without a trace of a smile to his boss. "You are to be crowned king in November. It would be awkward if I should have to protect your unborn child until he or she is old enough to take your place."

Ivy felt such a hitch in her body she had to lay a hand over her middle to ease the tightness. It was as if the baby had heard and understood the importance of its existence. For the first time, the fact that her child was heir to a throne became real to her.

"But you would do it," Max said quietly.

"Yes," Chuck replied.

The depth of friendship and loyalty between the two men became evident by the simple exchange. When they both looked at her, she realized she was the center of their concern—she and the baby she carried. A tremor shook her to the core of her being.

"No one will hurt the child if I can prevent it," she said, joining in the pledge to protect the little one.

"Then you will do exactly as we say?" Max asked, pinning her with a hard stare.

She frowned, not sure what she was willing to commit herself to doing. "I'm not inclined to follow orders blindly, but I have given some thought to the situation."

She pushed her empty plate aside and poured a fresh cup of coffee from the room service cart.

"What was your conclusion?" Max asked, his eyes roaming over her in a sexy, lazy perusal. "By the way, Chuck, you should know that Ivy and I are engaged."

She started to deny it, but on second thought, decided that was what she'd agreed to. "A sort of trial engagement," she quickly clarified.

"A courtship, as it were," Max agreed. "Then we will be married at the end of the month."

"If it works out." She amended his statement to indicate it wasn't a sure thing.

Max grinned at her. His earlier kiss had nearly driven any idea of a platonic relationship right out of her mind.

"You are dangerously close to arrogance," she warned.

Chuck made a strangled sound, then laughed out loud. Max merely lifted his dark eyebrows in a definitely arrogant manner and finished his eggs and waffle.

"Anyway, I've thought about the listening devices." She looked at Chuck, all playfulness aside. "Someone could have searched my place looking for the educational system plans, specifically the new router design. Maybe they thought they could find out more by listening in on my calls. It wouldn't be the first time industrial espionage has been a factor in our company."

She paused, recalling the bitterness of her father over an employee who had taken a breakthrough discovery from Crosby Systems to their enemy, Terrence Logan. That technology had been worth millions of dollars and had doubled the market share of the Logan Corporation.

Chuck nodded. "I've talked to the assistant security chief in Lantanya. All is quiet and under control. The head of the national guard has finished the interrogation of the palace security force. Nothing new. I'm sure we have all the conspirators, or else I would never have left the country."

"Nor would I," Max said. "Not even for the rose."

When both men looked at Ivy, she became somewhat self-conscious. She assumed her code name was "the rose" with the security chief. Recalling the rose that Max had plucked for her and slipped into the bosom of her blouse, she couldn't prevent the wave of heat that swept into her face.

"I understand national security must come before all else," she told them. "I accept that."

"Good," Chuck declared with an approving nod. "I think we should discuss this with your brother. We may have to bring in the American FBI on the case."

"And the CIA, if it's determined to be an international affair," Max murmured, his manner one of deep thought. He glanced at Ivy. "If so, you will have no privacy, either from the government or the news media."

She nodded. At some point yesterday she had realized that in agreeing to a…a sort of trial engagement she had also agreed to all that went with being the fiancée of a prince.

Princess Ivy.

It sounded just too ridiculous! She pressed a hand to her throat, afraid of breaking into laughter at the ridiculous idea and not being able to stop.

Max touched her arm. "I will protect you as well as I can from those who will pester you for news and those who would harm you because of me."

"I know," she said softly, her heart swelling until it filled her with hope and eagerness and yearning. "I trust you." She glanced at Chuck. "I trust you both. I'll try to listen and follow your instructions about what is best, but I must be included in the planning and in the decision making."

When Chuck got up to answer the telephone, Max said for her ears alone, "It would be best if you shared a bed with me." He lifted her hand and kissed each knuckle, his smile teasing, his eyes daring her to deny it. "I will be assured of your safety that way."

"Platonic," she said firmly. "Sex complicates things."

"So you indicated last night," he said dryly, looking so grumpy she had to laugh.

She adopted a prim manner. "Putting off gratification is good for one's character, Your Highness."

"Or it may drive one to desperate acts," he retorted, and looked her over as if thinking of seizing her and making off for parts unknown.

Even if the danger was real, she thought, it was worth it for these moments and the closeness she felt to this man. She suddenly wanted to say yes to the marriage and to making love and to anything else he had in mind.

Ivy had a voice mail from Trent when she arrived at her office. "See me" was the terse message. She put her purse and jacket away, picked up a notepad and went to the CEO's office. The secretary waved her in as soon as she appeared.

In addition to her brother, Katie was there. Ivy was surprised. Was this a family meeting? Trent indicated she should close the door.

"Do you want coffee?" he asked after she'd greeted them and taken a seat in a leather chair next to Katie's.

"Please." She considered her tummy, which was acting up somewhat. Odd, but this week she'd felt more nauseated about an hour after breakfast than any other time. The only thing she was doing differently was taking a prenatal vitamin right after breakfast. "Do you have any crackers?" she asked. Those always made her feel better.

Trent gave her a sharp glance from shrewd brown eyes. Their father had trained him to take over the company, and her big brother had developed the necessary skills, including sizing up a situation on the spot.

"Are you pregnant?" he asked, getting right to the point of the meeting. He handed her a cup of coffee, then stood by the chair as if to mete out punishment.

She sighed. "Yes." The aroma of the coffee added to the turmoil in her stomach. "Crackers," she said.

Trent frowned, but went to his credenza. He opened a door and removed an acrylic canister filled with trail mix. He set it on the lamp table between her and Katie.

Ivy selected several pretzels and munched on those. "Ah," she said, feeling better at once, then realized her brother and sister were staring at her. "Is my being pregnant the topic of this meeting?" she asked, trying for a light tone, which was a success, and a smile, which wasn't.

"One of them," Trent told her.

He thrust a hand through his hair as he resumed his seat. Ivy tried to remember who also used that gesture, but it was only a fleeting thought. She had other things to deal with. "What are the others?"

"What is Max Hughes to you?"

Ivy glanced at Katie, who smiled solemnly but reassuringly at her. So Katie hadn't told all. That left it up to her. She hesitated, not sure where to begin.

With the night of grand passion nearly two months ago? No, that wasn't something she was prepared to discuss with her brother. She tried to think of a tactful beginning.

"Is he the father?" Trent demanded, sparing her the necessity.

"Yes."

"My God," her brother said in fatalistic tones.

Katie and Ivy glanced at each other uneasily. Ivy took a breath and prepared to tell him exactly who Max was.

Trent leaned forward. "Do you know who he is?"

"Who?" Ivy said, afraid he was going to announce that Max was an ax murderer or something equally awful.

"The king of Lantanya. Or he will be when he's officially crowned in November, I understand."

"Oh, well, yes, I know that."

"You went over there on business. For this company," Trent stated grimly. "And you slept with the king?"

"I didn't know that at the time."

"He told her he was Max Hughes, there on business the same as she was," Katie said, coming to her defense.

"How did you know about…the baby?" Ivy asked.

Rising, Trent paced to the window and turned, his dark blond hair backlighted by the sun into a halo effect. His face was grim. "Apparently everyone in the Western world knows. It's in all the tabloids that the royal prince is searching for his Cinderella, who ran off and left him with a broken heart."

"Oh" was all Ivy could say. The uncertainty of the past two months swept over her in a wave. She pressed a hand to her stomach and desperately reached into the snack jar with the other.

Trent came to her and dropped to his haunches. "I'm sorry," he said in a softer manner. "I didn't mean to browbeat you. It's just that…" He made a helpless gesture, as if words failed him.

Ivy could identify with that. "It's complicated," she finished his thought.

"Do tell." Trent gave her an ironic, albeit sympathetic, smile and returned to his seat. "So, little sis, what's next on your agenda?"

Katie spoke while Ivy tried to come up with an answer. "Max wants to marry her."

"And what do you want?" he asked Ivy.

She shrugged and ate another pretzel. "I don't know. He says we must marry. For the child. It's his heir and everyone in Lantanya knows, so… But I never thought…I mean, royalty and all that—"

"Princess Ivy," Katie broke in. "No! *Queen* Ivy! Oh, my gosh!"

Ivy nodded in despair. "I know. It makes no sense."

The intercom buzzed. With a glare at the interruption, Trent answered. "Yes?" Then, "Send him in," he said to his secretary. His eyes settled on Ivy. "Max is here."

Ivy had little time to prepare before Max was in the room, the door shut behind him. "Has Ivy told you her apartment was bugged?" he asked Trent.

Her brother looked thunderous as he muttered an expletive. "What else is going on that I don't know about?"

"That's what Chuck and I are trying to discover. Is this about me and Ivy? Or about Crosby Systems?"

"Or something entirely different that we haven't thought of," Katie added.

They all looked at her.

She held up her hands. "I don't know of anything, but we had better consider all the angles."

Max pulled up a chair and joined the group. Trent poured a cup of coffee and handed it across the desk. "Well, there was an attempt on my life in July. When Ivy was in my country," he added, his dark, exciting gaze on her.

"I heard about that." Trent gave the other man a hard stare. "Your uncle and a minister were arrested."

"And sentenced to life in prison."

Although Max spoke calmly, Ivy couldn't be so sanguine. "How dare they try to hurt you," she said, fierce and protective on his behalf.

He took her hand and brought it to his lips. "The rose shows her thorns," he declared softly, then released her.

"Is it safe for you to be out of the country?" Trent asked Max.

"Yes. In addition to the half brother, who is an acknowledged illegitimate son of my grandfather, my father had a younger brother. My uncle, Jean Claude Maxwell von Husden, is the minister of finance. He is a bulldog when it comes to the welfare of the kingdom."

"You can trust him?" Ivy demanded.

Max smiled gently at her. "Yes. He is the one who alerted me to possible trouble. Chuck already had his doubts about my half uncle's loyalty."

Ivy huffed in fury that his relative had wanted Max dead. Catching Katie's and Trent's eyes on her, she felt her cheeks grow warm while her heart knocked around her rib cage like a bumper car gone wacko.

Her brother steepled his fingers together as he thought. "There was another problem around the same time, maybe a little earlier," he said.

"Here at your company?" Max asked.

With a quick shake of his head, Trent explained. "It was something to do with that clinic where Ivy does volunteer work."

She drew back in surprise. "Children's Connection?"

"Yes," Trent said. "That case involved a foreign country, too. Russia. Someone tried to steal a baby from the adoptive mother, but the State Department intervened."

"How do you know this?" Max asked.

"From a friend. Miles Remington is on the board of the adoption agency. He was telling me about it recently."

"The agency handles adoptions from Russia?" Max obviously found this a bit odd.

"The government has clamped down on abortion as a means of birth control, I understand, so I imagine there are more babies available there now." Trent gestured to indicate he didn't know more.

"I can't see how that involves us." Max ran his gaze over Ivy. "Unless they're planning on stealing this baby when it comes…and that is a thing I won't allow."

A shiver of dread chased down Ivy's spine at his ominous tone. He was like a lion, the leader of his pack and its defender. He would be as fierce in battle as he was gentle in making love.

Clenching her teeth together, she frantically directed her mind to concentrate on the possible danger, not the all-too-definite passion.

Max directed his attention to Trent. "I want permission for my security chief to work directly with the head of Crosby Systems security. Chuck is sure we nipped the conspiracy in my country in the bud, as it were. I trust his judgment on this. Then probably company espionage accounts for the bug in Ivy's apartment."

"The new router software," Trent immediately said. "Ivy's team wrote a program that makes it the fastest networking system on the market now. There are other companies who'd like to get their hands on it."

"There was a sweep of your company over the weekend, Chuck says."

Trent nodded. "Company policy. We regularly

check all electronic lines and equipment. Plus, all computers with top-secret info are locked out of Internet connections where they can be hacked into."

Max glanced at Ivy. She nodded to indicate this was true. "Good," he said, rising. "I would like to speak to you," he said directly to her. "If your meeting is finished?" he added politely to her other family members.

"Yes," Trent said.

His smile surprised Ivy. There was a hint of amusement in it, as if he found the situation between her and Max humorous to some extent. But then his expression went stern as he directed a glare toward Max.

"We will need to discuss other things soon, I think," he said to Max. "Such as my expected nephew or niece."

Max stood when her brother did. "Ivy and I have agreed to an engagement," he informed the others coolly. "We shall marry by the end of the month."

Before she could do more than splutter indignantly, he ushered her from the room, down the hall and into her own office. There he backed her against the wall, crowding her with his much larger, stronger body.

"This is a trial engagement," she reminded him hotly, pressing her hands against his chest to hold him off.

"But it is an engagement." His eyes dared her to contradict him.

"While we get to know each other. While we see if this…if a relationship can work."

"It can," he assured her. "I think we know each other quite well, princess."

His grin stung her dignity. While that magical night had seemed right, even destined, now she was filled with doubts and indecision. She didn't understand how she, quiet, studious Ivy, could have behaved so recklessly.

"I want my child to be born here," she said stubbornly.

"That can be arranged. Chuck tells me the birthing facilities at Portland General are excellent."

His big hands glided up her arms, sending spirals of heat down into the inner core of her body. He leaned in close, so close she was surrounded by his aura.

"Don't," she whispered, aware that the office door was open, but more aware of his powerful nearness, the sheer masculinity of his presence and the hunger he incited in her.

"Don't touch you? Tell me not to breathe."

His breath of laughter stirred the hair at her temple. She felt his lips settle there and plant a gentle kiss, then another and another. Her mind went hazy. Thinking was soon going to become impossible.

"Max, this isn't… We shouldn't…"

When his hands closed over her waist, she stopped trying to speak. It was impossible anyway. Her lungs had stopped working.

"Ah, princess," he murmured, cupping his body into hers and pressing her lightly to the wall.

He was very definitely aroused, she found, as he shifted closer, ever closer. With a quick tug, he moved her hands from between them and up to his shoulders. Then his hands were on her again, one caressing her side while the other took possession of her breast.

With a gasp, she felt the beading of her nipple as a sharp contraction, a pang of excitement that shot all through her, making every nerve ending tingle.

"My sweet rose," he whispered, nibbling at her earlobe, then moving toward her mouth. "I've missed your taste, the sweet aroma of your body, the silk of your skin."

Suddenly he was no longer the mysterious prince, but Max, the man who had won her so completely one soft balmy night in summer when he'd romantically climbed a trellis and presented her with the most beautiful rose of all those growing there.

"Max," she said, not in protest nor denial, but need, hot and urgent and demanding. A tremor shook her all over.

His embrace tightened. She shifted, instinctively opening her legs a fraction. He slipped a foot between hers and caressed her with his whole body, keeping the delicious thrust of his passion light, teasing, driving her insane with hunger.

She heard laughter in the hall. "Max," she whispered in panic. "The door. Somebody—"

With a kiss, he cut off the frantic words. Reaching out, he shut the door and clicked the lock into place.

She clung to him, knowing this was madness but unable to refuse the wild rapture he stirred in her. The kiss, the caress went on and on. Their harsh, excited breathing was the only sound for long, long minutes.

At last he drew back. "You are a perfect lover," he told her after taking a deep breath. "You will also be a charming queen. And a wonderful mother to our children."

He left after promising to come by for her at quitting time. She sank into her desk chair, tired and disoriented and oddly deflated.

What about love? she wanted to ask. Didn't even a royal prince want love as well as desire?

Nine

Max drove Ivy to work on Wednesday morning. He asked permission to use her car while she was at her office.

"Of course," she replied, opening the car door.

"I'll be back for you at noon."

"Don't bother. I'm going to the hospital to rock the babies in the nursery. Katie can drop me off."

"What about lunch?"

"I'll pick up something in the cafeteria."

"Something healthy. Ned says you need to eat lots of fruits and vegetables."

She paused at the curb and gave him a questioning look. "Ned who?"

"Ned Bartlett. My valet and good friend. I spoke with him last night. He's delighted about the child and was quite adamant that we should return home soon. He's a worrier and likes to keep an eye on things."

"I see."

Max knew she didn't, not really, but he let it pass. Instead he gazed at her for one lingering moment, taking in the lovely picture she made in a pantsuit of deep bronze suede, a russet sweater and a scarf printed with fall leaves that repeated those colors plus added a bit of blue to go with her eyes.

"I'll see you at four, if not sooner," he promised.

"I work until five."

"You told the doctor at the hospital that you had an appointment with him today. It was on the calendar in your kitchen. Four o'clock."

"I'd forgotten," she admitted. "So much seems to have happened since then."

He nodded as she closed the car door and walked up the sidewalk. After waving when she glanced back, he waited until she was inside the lobby atrium of the Crosby building, glad that it required an identification badge to get past the security guards at every entrance. Then he headed for a meeting of his own.

An hour later he and Chuck sat down with the regional FBI chief, a dour man who was clearly displeased that a foreign head of state was in the country without advance notification. "This is somewhat irregular," he said.

Max spoke before Chuck could defend their actions. "My passport is in order," he informed the man coolly. "I'm here on personal business, not state affairs."

"Ivy Crosby," the chief stated. His smile was dry. "I read the tabloids."

"And had us checked out after I contacted your office yesterday," Chuck added.

"True. The State Department is busy with other things at present. They have chosen to respect your request for privacy." The older man paused, then said, "Is there anything else I need to know about your visit?"

"Not that I know of," Max replied.

The FBI chief stood. "I hope you'll let me know when congratulations are in order."

"Of course." Max rose and shook his hand. "Thank you for your cooperation."

Once they were outside, Chuck frowned. "I thought we were going to bring the FBI into the picture."

"I've had second thoughts. Between us, Trent and his security men, we should be able to protect Ivy. If we have a couple of FBI agents hanging around, too, we may spook the enemy. Whoever that is."

"So what's the next step?"

Max checked the time. "I'm off to the hospital nursery to rock babies."

Chuck cast a doubtful glance his way, then smiled as if waiting for the punch line of a joke.

"I am," Max said, confirming his plans, then chuckled. "It's part of the courtship. I think I need to know more about babies, don't you?"

"Huh," Chuck snorted and shook his head. "It must be love."

"It will be," Max assured him. "It will be."

"You're determined to make her fall for you. Is that the plan, Your Highness?"

"Absolutely."

"Be careful you don't get caught in your own sticky web," the security chief advised, a knowing grin tucked into the corners of his mouth. He waved one hand in farewell and strode toward the rental car.

Max headed for the interstate highway, his pulse quickening at the thought of seeing Ivy. He mused over that, then shrugged. His father had explained that the impulses of youth were fleeting and that sex could lead one to false conclusions. A marriage, he'd said, was built a day at a time, like a castle, each stone adding to a strong foundation of trust and mutual respect that would last a whole lifetime.

Ivy had shown her trust in many ways, did she but know it. His trust in her was total.

At the hospital he parked in visitor parking and entered the lobby. There he found the usual confusing array of signs with directional arrows. He followed one that pointed down a corridor to the nursery wing after showing his ID to the security officer and mentioning his fiancée's name.

Soon he stood before a window behind which were a dozen or so clear plastic baby beds with wheels on the legs. Most of them were filled with babies in various stages of awareness—some sleeping deeply, some looking around and two crying, sounding desperately angry at the world.

The side wall of the nursery had a large plate-glass window the same as the one he peered through. In the adjoining room, he spotted Ivy with a baby in her arms.

His insides clenched in a funny way. Aware of a foolish grin that he couldn't suppress, he went to the door down the corridor and opened it. The baby on her shoulder slept peacefully. The one in her lap cried loudly.

"Hello. Would you like some help?" he asked.

The delighted expression on Ivy's face was enough to make him walk over hot coals to see it again.

"Yes. Come in."

He entered the small room, whose furniture consisted mostly of rocking chairs, and removed his suit jacket. "Tell me what to do," he invited.

"Choose a chair. I'll give you a baby." She frowned thoughtfully at him. "If you're sure you want to do this."

"I'm sure. I figure I'll need the experience."

She hesitated a second longer, then lifted the crying child onto her right arm while holding the other with her left. She gave him the squalling one, then put the other in one of the rolling bassinets.

"Uh, what do I do?" he asked, no longer sure about this experiment.

"I'll fix a bottle." She returned the sleeping infant to the other room, then prepared a bottle for his.

As soon as he plopped the nipple into the open mouth, the baby shut up and started sucking vigorously.

"Ah, that's more like it, old boy," he said, pleased with his success.

Ivy gave a little laugh, then laid a cloth over his left shoulder and tucked it between him and the child. "In case she spits up," she explained.

Max peered at the child as it drank, a wave of undefined emotion wafting through him. Knowing it was a girl changed his perspective on the baby. From the strength of its furious squalls, he'd assumed it was a boy.

He acknowledged his somewhat sexist assumption with a smile. The baby stopped sucking and stared at him. Then its tiny mouth trembled before it widened into a milky grin.

Without pausing to think, he grinned back.

The baby grinned some more, then started sucking again, its eyes never wavering from his face.

"She's fallen for you," Ivy murmured, leaning over his right shoulder, her breath caressing his temple. "I haven't seen her smile like that for anyone else."

"I think I've fallen for her, too," he admitted.

"She's one of our crack babies. It's a miracle she's made it this far. She was so tiny when she was born."

He caressed Ivy's cheek with his. "The instinct for survival is strong. How old is she now?"

"Four months. The volunteers have rocked and sung to her almost continuously during that time. I think she's going to be normal…"

Max glanced at Ivy as her voice trailed off, worry in her beautiful blue eyes. He realized she was thinking of the baby she carried. "Our child will be fine. You're healthy. So am I. Our baby will be, too."

He missed her warmth when she moved away. "Most babies are. It's just that since I've been coming here I've seen complications crop up that no one expected. It makes one rather uncertain." She sighed.

"Life doesn't come with a warranty," he told her softly as the child he held drifted into sleep. "We take it as it comes and work together to make something good."

She brought in another baby and started it on a bottle. "I wish I had your confidence."

"You trust me with your body," he told her. "Someday you'll trust me with your heart."

Her quick glance was wary. "Will you trust me with yours?" she asked, then began to rock gently, not expecting an answer.

"I already do," he said.

Their eyes met and held for a long minute before she looked away. Max shifted the baby a bit. The tiny girl opened her smoky-blue eyes, gave him another trust-filled smile and went back to sleep. His heart did an odd flip. He brushed the infant's cheek with the back of one finger, marveling at how small she was, how perfect.

Ivy laughed softly. "Watch it," she warned. "You *are* in danger of falling in love."

"Not me," he answered in the same playful tone she'd used. "Macho men are tough to the core."

The opening of the hall door disrupted the moment. Max swung his head around, smoothing out the frown of annoyance as he did. Another man stood there.

"Uh, I was just passing by," the stranger said.

"Everett," Ivy greeted the other man warmly. "Do come in. You must have known we needed you today. Max and I are the only two who showed up. Sit down. I'll give you this sleepyhead and try to soothe the screamer in there."

Max managed a smile when Ivy introduced the accountant from the adoption agency that was next door and was connected to the hospital in some way. Chuck had mentioned the place.

"It's called Children's Connection," Ivy said, finishing her explanation of Everett Baker's position there. "I haven't seen Nancy today," she told Everett.

Max watched with interest as the man became flustered at the mention of the woman.

"I, uh, wasn't here to see her," Everett said.

He sat in a rocker and gingerly accepted the baby Ivy placed in his arms and the bottle along with it. Poor guy. He looked about as comfortable as a nervous missionary trying to convert a tribe of cannibals.

"This is my first time, too," Max confided to the man while Ivy bustled into the nursery and retrieved a crying infant. "Smile at 'em. They seem to like that."

Ivy returned and soon had her baby quiet. "Everett has volunteered to help us before. This is his second time."

"Huh." Max didn't think the nerdy accountant

had gained much skill from his first visit. Smiling at his charming, sleeping baby, he thought he must have a knack for handling them. Dogs and cats had always liked him, too.

At that moment, an odd noise came from the tiny girl. She opened her eyes, squinted as if concentrating on a difficult subject, then made several more suspicious sounds. An unpleasant odor filled the room.

"Ivy," he said in alarm.

"I'll switch with you."

Max was relieved when she did. He continued feeding the other baby. He checked the wrist bracelet. A boy. Joshua.

"Hey, little man," he said when the boy opened his eyes and stared at him. Max gave him a smile.

The baby's chin wobbled, then he drew his legs up toward his chest. Next he thrust them straight and let out a yell like bloody murder. Max was so startled he nearly dropped both baby and the odd-looking bottle containing the plastic pouch of milk.

"What did you do, pinch him?" Ivy scolded a couple of seconds later. There was laughter in her eyes.

Max gladly exchanged the screaming Joshua with—he peeked at the name tag—Madison, Female. "What kind of name is that for a girl?" he asked.

The baby yawned and closed her eyes, totally secure in her tiny world.

Like the Grinch, Max felt his heart grow three sizes.

On her way to Crosby Systems shortly after one Ivy stopped by one of the superstores that seemed to be cropping up all over. She parked Katie's car, which she'd borrowed since her sister was tied up in meetings, a good distance from the entrance doors so she'd get some exercise.

Walking through the pleasant September sunlight, she considered the warm feelings inspired by Max and the babies. It would be very easy to fall in love with him. He could "charm the devil out of his pitch-fork" when he put his mind to it, as an elderly neighbor had once said about her father.

Cutting across a line of parked cars, Ivy noticed another car pull into the parking lot, going very slowly as if looking for someone.

A warning ran along her nerves. She'd seen a similar vehicle at the hospital with two men sitting in it. She'd assumed they were waiting for someone who was visiting a patient or seeing a doctor.

Ducking behind a pickup, she noted there were two men inside the dark, late-model sedan. Were they following her?

Silly, she scolded her runaway imagination. One of them probably had to get something for his wife.

Going inside the huge store, she picked up the boxed pasta platter and tongs that were the day's special and hurried to the checkout line.

Two men in dark suits entered the store. They were talking in a relaxed fashion, but they were looking the place over as they walked. Again she felt a funny tingle along her nerves.

She recalled Max telling her that Chuck believed in following his gut instinct. Her gut felt very uneasy.

Taking a calming breath, she muttered, "Darn," as if she'd forgotten something and left her place in line. A plan had already formed in her mind.

She headed for the garden shop, laying the pasta platter on a shelf of welcome mats before exiting the main building. Outside, in a fenced area that contained plants and yard furniture, she slipped on sunglasses and pretended to consider the redwood trellises. In reality she was checking the aisle she'd come down before going outside.

No sign of the two men. They were probably casing the store, looking for her. Or picking up diapers as instructed by their wives.

Feeling foolish, she walked past the cashier near the open gate, gave the woman a smile, then went into the parking lot. Keeping cars between her and the building as much as possible, she walked fast but didn't run.

Relief filled her when she saw a large motor home pull across two parking spaces and hide her car from view. She crossed the open lane, dodged behind the motor home and unlocked Katie's compact car with shaking hands.

The dark-blue sedan was still in its place when she drove carefully away from the store. She didn't, however, see the men. Nor did she spot the car in her rearview on the way to Crosby Systems.

Ivy found Katie on the phone when she entered her sister's office and laid the car keys on the desk. Katie smiled and waved her to a chair.

Inside the building Ivy felt safe. Thanks to a security system that didn't allow anyone into the building without a guard's scrutiny, she thought as she sank into the cushions.

"What's happening?" Katie asked immediately upon hanging up the phone.

Ivy shrugged. "I'm not sure. I thought I was being followed." She explained what had happened. "It's probably nothing," she concluded.

"An overactive imagination? I don't know." Katie was silent as she considered the possibilities. "This appears to be connected to Max, don't you think? Nothing suspicious occurred until he arrived in town."

An ill feeling swept through Ivy at the thought that he might still be in danger. She wrapped her arms across her tummy until the fear dissolved.

"So, you do care," Katie murmured.

"Of course. I don't want him to be hurt because of me. Because he followed me here," she amended.

Katie pushed her glasses up on her nose, her eyebrows raised as she studied Ivy. "Is that all?" she asked softly.

"Yes," Ivy said at once, then, "I don't know. He isn't the person I thought he was."

"Who is?" Katie questioned sardonically.

Ivy leaned an elbow on the chair and propped her chin on her palm. "Being a prince is a lot different from being a businessman, though. Intrigues. Absurd tabloid stories. Your every move recorded."

"Poor Max. I wonder how he stands it. Life in a fish bowl must be terribly lonely. Especially when you're the only fish in it," Katie added softly.

"He said even royalty needed private moments."

Moments to cherish, he'd told her. With her. With their children. And with friends. She sighed shakily.

"Of course." Katie nodded as if she understood completely and totally agreed.

"So you think I should marry him?"

Katie studied her a long moment. "That's up to you, little sister. Max seems honorable. I think you can trust him. But only you know your own heart."

But that was the problem, Ivy mused later in her office. Her heart wasn't very reliable. She turned on her computer and began reading the e-mails, bringing her mind firmly back to work-related matters.

At twenty of four, Max strolled into her office. She noted he had a photo badge, which allowed him to wander about the place without an escort.

"Your brother provided it," he told her, seeing her glance at the ID tag.

"A good idea since you're determined to make a nuisance of yourself."

His laughter did things to her insides. She sternly quelled the desire to rush to his arms and kiss him until they were both senseless. "Let's go."

He was obviously amused about something as she directed him to the clinic near the hospital. He kept giving her oblique glances as he drove. Once, he shook his head slightly.

"What's so funny?" she asked.

"Something Chuck told me." He parked in an open slot at the medical clinic.

"About me?"

"About how evasive a woman could be if she set her mind to it."

At the door to the doctor's office, she stopped in her tracks. "Those men," she said. "They were sent by Chuck, weren't they?"

Max had the audacity to laugh. "You outwitted two of Crosby Systems' best security detectives. How did you get out of the store?"

"Through the garden shop. It has a gate that opens on the parking lot."

"When did you spot them?"

"I saw them sitting in their car at the hospital when I left. I thought they were waiting for someone. But when they arrived at the store where I stopped, I became suspicious. I mean, two men in business suits being at the same places I was without any apparent reason..." She shrugged one shoulder. "It didn't seem likely."

"I'll warn Chuck about that."

"Warn him not to have me followed," she said hotly. "That's unnecessary. Besides, it scared me. I thought they were after me because they wanted to get to you."

The laughter disappeared from his handsome face. His eyes became dark and deep and questioning as he gazed into hers. "Ivy," he said, his tone husky and very tender.

Returning his stare, Ivy experienced the classic symptoms of falling in love—breath shortening, heart beating hard, vision narrowing until he filled her world—

Just then the door was pulled open from inside, startling her and destroying the moment.

"Oh! I'm sorry. I didn't realize anyone was there," a very pregnant woman exclaimed.

"No, it was my fault," Ivy told her. She and Max stepped aside so the woman could leave, then went inside the modern office decorated in green and mauve. After signing in, she sat on the green chenille sofa with thin mauve strips and worried about the tumult raging inside her.

"Don't worry so," Max murmured for her ears only. "You'll make the baby anxious."

She gave him a challenging glance. "You know so much about it?"

"I've been reading up on child rearing," he said virtuously. He picked up a parenting magazine. "Ah, this looks like an interesting article."

She glanced at the title he pointed out. The Emotional Ups and Downs of Pregnancy and Birth. She met his eyes, then laughed. "I can vouch for that."

When her name was called, Max rose and went into the inner office with her. Ivy noted a couple of women looking at her with envy. If they only knew the whole story, she thought, would they be shocked or intrigued?

Studying him surreptitiously, she got her answer easily. He was the most fascinating person she'd ever met.

The nurse gave her the usual paper gown after taking her vital signs and writing them on the chart. "Uh, do you want to wait in the doctor's office?" she asked Max.

"No." He crossed his arms and planted his feet as if taking a firm stand.

"It's okay," Ivy said quickly before the motherly looking woman could argue with him. Ivy pulled the curtain across the dressing area in the corner of the room and changed to the gown. Then she sat on the end of the exam table. They waited in silence.

"I think we've met before," the doctor said, smiling as he entered the room. He shook hands with Max. "Dan Woodruff."

"At the hospital last week," Max affirmed. "I'm Max Hughes."

The doctor took a seat on a stool and motioned Max to the chair. He looked over her chart and asked some questions on her recent health. "Do you want me to deliver or would you like a referral to an obstetrician? We have several good ones in the clinic."

"I'd rather stay with you," Ivy said. When Max would have said something, she shook her head. "He's been my doctor for ten years. I'm comfortable with him."

Max sized up the youthful-looking doctor. "How long have you been in practice?"

"Ten years." He smiled, showing a perfect set of white, even teeth. "Ivy was one of my first patients. She recommended me to all her friends and family."

"I see."

Max shot her a keen glance, which made Ivy feel defensive as if he questioned her motives. Well, she'd had a slight crush on the doctor for a year or so. All her friends had. Then he'd married another doctor.

"His wife is in pediatrics," she explained.

Max smiled. "Good."

Ivy rolled her eyes.

"Let's figure out your due date," Dr. Woodruff suggested. "Do you know when you conceived?"

A lump formed in her throat. Before she could clear it and speak, Max said with great certainty, "July eighteenth."

"Hmm, a Friday," the doctor noted, looking at the calendar on the side table.

"That should make her due in April, right?" Max asked.

"Right. Human gestation is around 280 days. Let's see…" He figured it out. "April twenty-third should be it."

"How long after the birth before Ivy and the child can travel?"

The doctor and Ivy stared at him.

Max took her hand. "We will need to return to Lantanya within six weeks for the official christening."

"Lantanya?" the doctor inquired.

"My country. We will live there most of the year. With frequent visits to your family," he said to Ivy. "I wouldn't separate you from Trent and Katie. I know you're close."

Tears stung Ivy's eyes. He was wonderful in so many ways. If only he were a simple businessman, she would marry him without a qualm. But he wasn't. She blinked back the useless tears.

Dr. Woodruff glanced at her ring finger. "You are married or planning on it soon?"

To her surprise Max turned to her, waiting with the doctor for her answer. "We're engaged," she finally said.

"We hope to marry by the end of the month," Max added.

She wondered if he used the imperial *we* of kings or if he had made the assumption she was of the same hope. She realized the idea wasn't quite as shocking as it had been a week ago.

The doctor laid the chart aside. "Okay, let's see how you're getting along." He turned to Max. "My office is one door down. Wait there for us."

The examination proceeded, then ended with a sonogram. Max was invited in to view the fetus.

Later, telling Chuck about the experience during dinner at the hotel suite, he remarked, "It looked like a cross between a tadpole and a seahorse." He flashed Ivy a teasing grin.

She gave him a mock-indignant glare, then thought about the developing child, wondering whether it was a girl or a boy. And what its life would be.

At ten she turned in, alone in the king-size bed. She heard the drone of the men's voices in the living room for a while. Chuck had been rather put out that she'd detected the detectives.

Max had reminded him that Ivy had a sharp mind and noticed things. He'd seemed rather proud of her.

At last all was quiet. She slept, then awoke, restless from dreams she didn't recall. Rising, she slipped on a robe and crept silently into the living room. Max lay at an angle under the sheet on the sofa bed. The bed was barely long enough for him.

Gazing at him in the pool of moonlight from the open curtains, she realized his eyes were open. He smiled when he saw that she knew he was awake.

"Join me," he invited on a lazy note.

"You can join me," she said.

He rose at once. She saw he wore sweatpants, which surprised her for some reason. But she'd only seen him when he'd been in bed with her, when neither had worn night clothes.

Taking her hand, he let her lead the way into the bedroom, then closed the door behind them.

"Is this platonic?" he asked.

She hesitated a fraction of a second. "Only if you want it to be."

He caught her to him. "You have no idea how I want it to be," he murmured, "but I'll show you."

With the gentlest of touches, with kisses so sweet they melted her heart, he made love to her as if they had all the time in the world.

When the sensation became unbearable, she sobbed in his arms as ecstasy flowed over her, through her, piercing all the secret places of longing she'd ever known.

"I love you," she said, unable to stop the words. "I love you, love you, love you."

Ten

Max was on the phone when Chuck entered the suite, jogging clothes damp from his exercise. He returned Chuck's wave, then continued his conversation with Ned, who was at the palace in Lantanya.

"Talk to the architect," he told his valet and friend, "and let's see what we can come up with. My wife and I will share a bedroom. She'll want the nursery nearby. I'm thinking of the suite across the hall from mine for the children."

"Very good, Your Highness," Ned said, sounding both surprised and pleased.

Max smiled. Perhaps he was being premature, but after last night he decided to proceed as if the marriage at the end of the month was a set-in-stone fact. Which it was, as far as he was concerned.

Warmth spread through him, heating his blood and firing his imagination. No, not imagination, his memories. Last night Ivy had been incredible in her response. Now past most of her original shyness, she'd been pleasingly aggressive and demanding, every man's dream of a perfect lover.

I love you, love you, love you.

The words she'd murmured during the excitement of their desire had filled him with added pleasure. A bonus. He'd slept in deep contentment with her in his arms.

This morning she'd been introspective while dressing for work, but she hadn't attempted to deny the words she'd whispered at the height of passion. The contentment filled him again. He'd never known anything like it—

"You look like the cartoon cat who has at last caught the pesky mouse," Chuck said, interrupting his thoughts. "Did I hear you talking to Ned? Is there anything that needs my attention?"

"I'm making a few modifications on the family living quarters. Ivy will want our children close, so I'm having the nursery moved across the hall."

"To the queen dowager suite?"

"Yes. Since my mother is dead, there's no need for it."

"The marriage is definitely on, then?"

Max met his friend's amused but serious gaze. "Yes. I think we can assume all is well in that department."

Chuck's cool blue eyes lingered on the sofa bed. The maid hadn't yet been in to straighten and tuck it out of sight. Max, to his amazement, felt his ears grow hot.

"I thought so when I didn't find you up and ready to go for a run this morning." His friend hesitated, then added softly, "I'm happy for you, Max. Ivy is a fine woman."

Max nodded. "She is that."

I love you, love you, love you.

He suddenly wanted very much to hear those words again, not in passion this time, but in total trust and endearing honesty. His throat closed up and he felt that odd flip of the heart he'd experienced while holding the baby.

"Taking on the responsibilities of a wife and children makes a man view life differently," he confided to his best friend. "The future becomes much more real."

"It'll be good to get this settled before you have to assume the mantle of king. You'll need a place to rest, someone special to come home to, as it were."

"Private moments," Max murmured.

"Will Ned's wife assist Ivy? As queen, she'll need a personal maid to take care of her clothing. I like the idea of having an older woman experienced in palace protocol, someone discreet as well as trustworthy."

"Mrs. Bartlett has two children of her own."

"Both nearly grown. She'll like having new babies to spoil, or so she told me back in the spring."

"Oh, she did, did she?" Max chuckled, then poured another cup of coffee and pushed the pot across the table to Chuck. "We'll need a security escort for Ivy at all times."

"Also the children," Chuck added. "Don't worry. I'll see that they have the best. No one will hurt them."

A whirl of emotion so strong it was almost painful speared through Max at the thought. "It's a different realm," he said, "this marriage and family business. I'm not sure I'm trained for it. To be a king, yes. To be a husband…" He frowned at the uncertainty that dogged him of late.

The two friends sat in silent contemplation of the coming changes, then Chuck smiled. "I think you'll get the hang of it, old chum." He lifted his coffee cup in a salute, then removed a sheaf of papers from a folder he'd laid on the table earlier. "Here are the latest reports from the diplomatic courier this morning. All is calm in the kingdom, according to the department ministers and captain of the palace guard. My security men agree."

"So does Ned," Max commented.

"Then," said Chuck, "all is right with the world."

"Or will be, once the rose and I are married," Max said thoughtfully. He took a deep breath and let it out slowly. Thank God that was settled. He hadn't known it was a weight on his shoulders until last night when it had rolled away sometime during their idyllic moments together.

Ivy was hard at work reviewing the Lantanya project when Trent stalked into her office. "Hi," she said. "Did you know we have another delay from production? I'm beginning to worry about meeting our deadlines."

Trent closed her door with a bang. "I'm worried about *you*. The head of security says you eluded the two men assigned to stay with you."

Ivy stood and looked her brother in the eye. "If I'd known they were my guards, I might not have eluded them. Or been scared out of my wits."

"Why didn't you use your cell phone and call somebody to ask what was going on instead of pulling the female James Bond trick?"

"I didn't think of it," she snapped. "I was too busy trying to escape. I didn't have time to call everyone I knew and ask if they happened to have two men tailing me, thank you very much!"

They glared at each other until Ivy realized how much alike they looked with their chins out and their hands on their hips. The corners of her mouth twitched, then broke into a grin.

Trent grimaced, then gave a faint smile. "Okay, this is getting too much like a TV drama. Why don't you marry your prince and get out of the country while I figure out what's going on?"

"You think it has to do with Crosby Systems, then?"

"What else can it be?" He paced to the window.

Ivy stood beside him, her gaze following his to the perfectly landscaped lawn in front of the building. All was beautiful and serene out there. She sighed and settled into her chair.

"I don't know," she said. "Things feel funny. Out of kilter somehow."

"Woman's intuition?" His tone was gently mocking.

"I suppose." She paused. "I think Max and I will be wed soon. A small wedding with family and close friends."

"So you've decided." He laughed. "I'm surprised Max let you come back to work once you agreed. If I were in his shoes I'd whisk you off to the preacher ASAP."

Ivy lifted her chin. "I won't be rushed into anything. Besides, I haven't exactly told him yet."

Trent's eyebrows rose in question.

"Tonight," she said on a half note of promise. "Or tomorrow. Definitely before the end of the week."

His expression became somber. "Are you sure this is what you want?"

She hesitated. Images of the night spent in Max's strong, gentle arms whirled around her. He'd been tender and fierce in his passion, and generous, making sure of her satisfaction before taking his own. They'd spent a total of three nights together, each one better than the last. Practice did indeed make perfect.

"Well?" Trent demanded, shaking her from her reverie.

"Yes," she said softly, "this is what I want."

Trent looked pleased. "Good. It's settled then. Today is Thursday. Do you want the wedding on Sunday? I think we can arrange it."

She held up a hand to stop his hurried planning. "Wait! I'm just getting used to the idea of an actual marriage." She checked the calendar. "How about the following Sunday? That's the twenty-first. I need to find a dress and arrange for flowers. I love mums, so we can have those for a fall wedding. Then there's food for the reception."

"I'll have my secretary call the country club and arrange all that. We can do the reception there. Dad and the company can foot the bill."

Ivy gave him a frown. "I thought we said a small wedding. Everyone we know will be at the country club if this gets out."

"A small wedding, yes, but the reception will have to be much larger. There'll be publicity whether we want it or not. Our largest business associates will expect to attend. Maybe this will smoke out whoever is trying to steal our secrets. I'll call Chuck and alert him. Hey, you think he would like to work for our company?"

Without waiting for an answer, Trent headed to his office, his mind obviously buzzing with details, while Ivy sank weakly against the chair back, her train of thought a total wreck of half-formed plans, fears and hopes.

When her phone rang, she answered rather absently.

It was Katie. "Ivy, Trent just told me the news. Am I going to be your best woman?"

"Of course. You and Emma. I'll call her. No, no, I have to call Max first. He won't like reading about the plans for the ceremony in the headlines of a tabloid."

She told Katie she wanted the wedding to be outside. The maple and alder trees on her father's estate were simply beautiful as they changed to fall colors.

"Then that's where it'll be," Katie declared. "With white and golden mums lining the gazebo, it'll be lovely. Our stepmama will be thrilled. She loves to plan a party."

"So does our mom."

There was a beat of silence as if Katie had forgotten about Sheila. "Yeah, she'll want to be the center of attention. Maybe we can distract her somehow."

"Max can handle her." Ivy pressed a hand to her forehead. "No more. I've got to get in touch with Max."

"No problem," Katie said. "He just walked by my door and is heading your way."

"Thanks for the warning. Talk to you later." Ivy hung up and composed herself as much as she could with her heart sounding like the 110 trombones of song.

Max, her heart sang. *Max, my love.*

She flew to his arms when he came into the room.

The rest of Thursday and all of Friday passed in a rush of activity and emotion as Ivy told her parents and siblings of the plans. Late Friday afternoon she and Katie went shopping for wedding finery.

Ivy was willing to settle on the first dress she tried on, but Katie insisted they check several stores. Four hours later they went back and bought the first wedding gown and left with promises that it would be hemmed by Tuesday. Ivy also selected a long dress made in a coordinating style for Katie. The russet shade was wonderful with her sister's skin tones, brown eyes and sun-streaked brown hair.

Max had agreed to Ivy's plans without objection. "But you do realize we will have to have a formal ceremony in my country?" he asked Friday night as they lay entwined in the king-size bed.

"No. Why?"

"Tradition. The royalty of Lantanya are wed in the cathedral so that everyone can see they are truly bonded and their children are legitimate."

Ivy laid a hand over her abdomen with a tired sigh. "That means more shopping. Will we have to stand in a reception line for hours the way Queen Elizabeth did?"

"Yes, but I will see that you don't become fatigued. No harm will come to the child," he averred.

"Thank you," she said, snuggling against him.

"We will have the ceremony immediately after the coronation, then as king, I will crown you as my queen."

Ivy started to protest that she needed more time to think about this, then she realized it was too late. The wheels for the royal marriage were already in motion.

"I will do my best," she said simply, gazing into his dark eyes.

"Ah, Ivy, you please me in so many ways. The day we met, my ministers had already told me much about you, that you were polite and intelligent and knowledgeable in your dealings with them. I've found you to be kindhearted and generous, a person of integrity…and passion."

With a chuckle he seized her and proceeded to let

her have her way with him. Ivy found the weariness of shopping disappeared with a little TLC. She awoke refreshed on Saturday morning.

"What are your plans for the day?" Max asked over coffee at the breakfast table.

Ivy was aware of his and Chuck's eyes on her while she swallowed a sip of coffee before answering. It came to her that their lives would always be shared with others, such as Chuck and Ned and palace officials. Except for the few hours they would have in privacy in their bedroom. A cold sensation trickled down her spine.

"I'm going to the nursery to rock the babies this morning," she told the men. "Katie and I are meeting for lunch with the florist at noon, then I'm supposed to go to the country club to talk to the coordinator about the reception at two. Oh, and I have to call Emma to see if she can be the matron of honor."

"No flower girls and ring bearers?" Max asked, his eyes gleaming in sardonic humor as he teased her.

"No. Since neither of us has nieces or nephews, that won't be necessary. Thank goodness," she added. "At least with a quick wedding, I won't have time for a nervous breakdown before it's over."

Both men roared at this conclusion, delivered in a deadpan voice. She smiled and rose. "Am I to have a bodyguard today?"

Max glanced at Chuck, then at Ivy. "Not if you'll agree to let one of us drive you to wherever you need to go."

"What about when I'm with Katie?"

"What do you think?" Max asked his security chief.

Chuck considered. "There haven't been any personal incidents and we've seen nothing suspicious since we found the bugs. So as long as you and your sister stay together and go only to restaurants and public places, I think it will be okay."

"No strange men sitting around in cars and trying to act invisible?" she asked.

Chuck grimaced at her amusement. "Not without telling you first," he said.

"Oh, joy. You guys are finally going to keep me in the loop." She gave them each a big approving smile and leaned over to smooch Max on the cheek. She stopped. "Am I allowed to kiss the king in front of someone else, Your Highness?"

"I'll show you," he growled and pulled her across his lap and kissed her until she was dizzy and could only cling to him as her breath hung someplace in her throat.

Then he set her on her feet. "Ready to go?"

"I'm not sure. I'm still dizzy."

Laughing, Max put an arm around her and guided her to the door, grabbing her purse and handing it to her as they went. "I'll be back in twenty minutes," he told Chuck.

"I have some calls to make. The FBI and the U.S. State Department will have to know about the wedding. The president might attend."

"Tell him he can come to the official ceremony in Lantanya. This one is for family only."

Ivy couldn't believe how cavalier he was, regarding the president of the United States. "You are incorrigible," she scolded as they walked down the hotel corridor.

"But you like my kisses," he whispered in the elevator as he nibbled on her ear.

"I do," she whispered back. "I do indeed."

"Yeah?"

"Uh, it's me."

"Make it quick. I'm expecting another call."

"There's to be a transfer today, around noon, from the hospital nursery over to Children's Connection nursery."

"Today? Why the hell didn't you let me know sooner? I can't get someone on it with no notice."

"Well, the mother didn't sign the adoption papers until an hour ago—"

"Great. You handle it."

"I, uh, can't. I'm at work. Besides, if I were recognized, we would lose the inside info."

"All right, all right, let me think. Okay, I can handle it. Give me a call when the transfer takes place."

"I can't use the office line. The call could be traced. I'm at a pay phone now. If you're here within an hour, that should be time enough."

"Damn. Where will the kid be?"

"The nurse will have to bring the baby to the reception area to sign it over to the adoption agency. I'll open and close the blinds on my office window when it arrives."

"Okay, we'll be there."

"Uh, who's we?"

"My ol' grandma. Don't ask any more stupid questions. We'll stay in the car until you give the signal."

"Good news," Matissa, the head nurse, told Ivy and Nancy at the hospital nursery. "The mother has decided to put this little one up for adoption." She glanced down at Madison. "We're getting her ready to go over to Children's Connection."

"What made her change her mind?" Ivy asked.

"She was told she'd have to take the baby home and that she needed to continue the rocking and special care for the foreseeable future. She started crying and said she had no place to go. The father would kick her out if she brought a 'squalling brat' home. He hadn't wanted it in the first place." The pediatrics nurse shook her head.

"Poor baby," Nancy murmured, her brown eyes tearing up as she patted the back of the little one she was holding.

Ivy picked up the infant who was making little sobbing sounds as she gazed forlornly at the ceiling. "Come on, sweetie, let's rock and talk it over."

After Madison quieted, Ivy gave her a bath and changed her into fresh clothing. She and Nancy helped bathe the other babies while Matissa recorded weight and food consumed and administered medication to those requiring it.

Ivy took a quick break at midmorning and spotted her good friend in the corridor. "Emma!" she called. When she caught up with the other woman, she added in a low voice, "I've been meaning to call you. I need a matron of honor for my wedding a week from Sunday. Think you can make it?"

Emma's eyes opened wide, then she gave Ivy a bear hug. "I've never known anyone who married a prince before. I read the front page of a tabloid at the grocery. It said he would be crowned king in November. Is that true?"

Ivy nodded. "Queen Ivy. Can you imagine?" she said with a sardonic roll of her eyes.

"It's incredibly romantic. But," Emma told her firmly, "the most important thing is that you two be happy together. Remember that when things get rough."

"I will," Ivy promised.

A nurse stepped out of a room. "Mrs. Davis, your room is ready now."

"Thank you," Emma said.

Ivy noticed the overnight case Emma held. "What's going on? Are you being admitted?" She followed the other woman into the private room.

Emma nodded. "It's nothing serious. I'm having a laparoscopy this afternoon."

"For the endometriosis? Why didn't you let me know it was going to be this soon?"

"I tried to call but got no answer. I left word on your answering machine."

"Oh, Em, I'm so sorry! I haven't been home in a couple of days." When her friend glanced at her in question, Ivy explained, "I'm staying at the hotel with Max and Chuck." She waited until the nurse left the room. "Someone broke into my apartment the other day. So much has been happening this month."

She realized it was only the thirteenth of September, that less than two weeks had passed since she'd bought the pregnancy test and confirmed her suspicions.

Concern for her friend overrode her thoughts. "Will the surgery increase your chances of carrying a baby to term?" she asked.

"Yes, by about twenty-five percent. It's a long shot, but…" Emma shrugged and gave her a faint smile.

"It'll be worth it. You and Morgan will make wonderful parents. How long will you be in the hospital?"

"Twenty-four hours. You know how they throw you out at the first opportunity."

This last was said with a grin at the motherly nurse who had returned with a hospital gown, a box of tissues, towels and other paraphernalia. "We can't have sick people lollygagging around here all the time," she declared.

After laughing and chatting a couple more minutes, Ivy returned to her duties in the nursery. Nancy Allen was still there, holding Joshua and singing to him slightly off-key.

"Do you have duty today?" Ivy asked the E.R. nurse.

She shook her head. "I'm free all weekend. In every way," she added.

Ivy took a baby and its bottle from the head nurse and settled in a rocker. "Aren't you and Everett dating anymore?"

"I guess not. If we ever were," she added dismally.

Ivy gave her a sympathetic glance.

"Women and babies seem to frighten him in equal amounts." Nancy bounced Joshua when he stirred. He settled back into sleep and she continued to rock him.

"I'm thirty-one," Nancy confided. "That's not old by today's standards, yet I'm feeling the press of time and not having a family or at least someone special—" She broke off with a laugh. "Alas, poor me."

Ivy nodded. "I know exactly what you mean. All my friends were so into relationships when we were in college, but I didn't find anyone who made the earth shake with his kisses, let alone someone interesting, to tell the truth."

"By the way, the newspaper had a small piece about how much the fund-raiser brought in. You and Hunter run an efficient bazaar," Nancy said.

"Yes, I was pleased with the final amount."

"I saw Hunter with his son yesterday going to the pediatrics clinic," Nancy said, switching subjects. "He brought the boy in for some tests, he said."

Ivy frowned. "He told me Johnny hasn't been feeling well, that he didn't have his usual energy. I hope it isn't anything serious."

"Hunter lost his wife not long after they adopted Johnny, didn't he?"

"Yes. It would be terrible if something happened to his son…" Ivy blinked away the sting of tears.

"Well, Matissa and I will be crying in our beer next," Nancy said. She adopted a lighter tone. "The latest news I heard was that you and your Prince Charming are getting married next Sunday. Is that true or just a rumor?"

"True. I think." Ivy pressed her free hand to her temple. "Everything is whirling faster and faster in my head. I keep expecting it to explode like a balloon from too much happening too fast." She sighed.

Matissa came to the door of the comforting room. "Ivy, do you have time to do me a favor?"

"Sure."

"Can you take Madison to the adoption agency? They're ready for her over there. They have a couple coming in this afternoon to see her. She's as ready as she'll ever be."

"That's wonderful. I would love to walk her over. Do you think it would be okay to take the long way across the lawn? It's so beautiful outside today. I think she would love to look at the world instead of hospital walls for a change, don't you?"

"That will be fine. I'll call and let them know you're on the way. I have her things all ready. There's a carriage for transport, so you don't have to schlep everything over like a pack mule." Matissa went to the telephone and punched in the adoption agency's number.

Ivy laid the sleepy baby in the carriage.

"Okay, you're clear," Matissa called out as soon

as she hung up the phone. "The receptionist has the papers to check the baby in. You'll need to sign that you delivered her to the agency."

"Right." Ivy turned to Nancy. "See you Monday. I won't be back later. Too many errands to run this afternoon."

"Take care," Nancy said. "You, too," she added with a sweet smile for the baby.

Ivy wheeled the carriage outside. The sun was bright and warm on her face. She inhaled deeply. The air was like ambrosia, filling her with a sense of well-being.

Flowers bloomed in lush profusion in beds across the lawn. Benches and tables were placed conveniently around, although none was occupied at present. The noon hour, when visitors and sometimes staff came outside to eat, was still several minutes away.

She turned onto a winding sidewalk that would take her to the front door of the annex that housed Children's Connection, a combination adoption agency and fertility clinic started by the efforts of the Logan family after Robbie Logan had disappeared.

She adjusted the carriage hood over the sleeping baby. Madison opened her eyes, looked around, spotted her and smiled. "You little doll," Ivy murmured.

A couple got out of a car parked at the curb. The woman was elderly. Her makeup was terrible and had been put on with a heavy hand. She wore a sweatsuit that was baggy at the knees and the kind of lace-up shoes that older women seemed to favor.

The man, who was probably her son, took her arm as they walked toward Ivy.

"Oh, what a darling baby," the woman said, stopping by the carriage. The man stopped, too, blocking the sidewalk.

Ivy smiled patiently as the woman talked softly to the darling little girl.

Before Ivy could guess at her intent, the grandmotherly woman leaned into the carriage. "I just love to hold babies," she said, reaching for Madison.

"I'm sorry, but you can't—"

Ivy broke off when the woman snatched the baby from the carriage. "You can't," she began again, then realized the couple were leaving—with the baby!

With a thrust of her arms, she pushed the carriage into the back of the woman's legs, causing her to stumble. Before the man could pause and turn, Ivy, in three strides, rescued the baby from the woman's clutches.

"Oh, no, you don't," the man growled and clamped a hand on her arm.

Ivy used the heel of one hand to whack him under the chin, forcing his head up and, she hoped, his teeth into his tongue. She sprinted for the agency when the man's hold loosened. Just as she was grabbed from behind, she spotted Morgan Davis, the director of the agency.

"Morgan, help! Kidnappers!"

It took him less than a second to assess the situation, then he was running across the lawn, trampling flower beds and leaping over a low boxwood hedge.

Ivy held on to the baby for dear life as the man tried to pry Madison out of her arms. Then he bought his fist up and hit her in the face. Stars literally danced before her eyes. The iron-tinged taste of blood filled her mouth, but she gritted her teeth and clung to the bundle in her arms.

"Get your hands off her!" Morgan yelled, coming at them like a locomotive at full thrust. "Everett, grab the woman!"

Ivy realized another man was coming to help. The woman kidnapper evaded the shy accountant and leaped into the car, locking the driver's door behind her. Everett rushed after Morgan to help subdue the man.

From behind her, Ivy heard a shout from the hospital emergency room portico. More help, thank goodness! She wasn't sure she could hold on much longer.

"Come on!" the woman shouted from the car, not acting at all like an elderly lady now. She pulled the vehicle forward until it was near her struggling accomplice.

The man gave Ivy a hateful snarl, then kicked her before he released her and ran. The woman sped off before he got the door of the old car completely closed.

Ivy went down with the blow to her abdomen, but managed to roll so she didn't crush the screaming baby she so desperately held. Morgan glared in frustration after the car, which turned the corner and sped out of sight. He knelt down. "Ivy, you okay?"

"I don't think so." Her breath was ragged. "Please, could you take the baby?"

Morgan did so, then another face loomed over her. "They're gone," Everett assured her, breathing hard. He'd chased the car a ways down the street before giving up.

"Thank you," Ivy said. "Thank you both." Then she moaned and wrapped her arms over her middle. "I think…I need…some help," she whispered as pain and fear in equal parts swept through her. "I need Max."

Eleven

The E.R. medic wouldn't let Ivy move until a gurney was brought down to where she lay on the sidewalk. She felt rather foolish as several anxious faces peered down at her.

"I can get up," she told them.

"We'll lift you," the medic said. He and Morgan and Everett lifted her onto the portable stretcher, then the medic wheeled her up to the emergency room. The on-duty doctor was ready and waiting for her. The older woman quickly checked Ivy's vital signs and listened to her heart after instructing the nurse to apply a cold pack to the bruise forming on Ivy's face.

"Any pain?" she asked, palpating Ivy's abdomen. "Other than the sock on the jaw, that is."

"There's some lower back pain, but otherwise I feel pretty good, considering."

The doctor examined the bruising on her face. "What did he hit you with?"

"His fist." Ivy held the pack in place while the nurse brought over an IV stand. "What's that for?"

"We're going to give you a little something to calm things down," the doctor replied. "Your blood pressure is a bit high, and you're having a few contractions."

Ivy placed a hand on her tummy. "Contractions? A miscarriage?"

"I don't think so." She gave instructions to the nurse.

In a couple of minutes, Ivy was in the stirrups, her anxiety increasing as the doctor checked her over thoroughly and announced that everything looked fine.

"I don't detect any amniotic leakage." She studied Ivy for a moment, then patted her shoulder. "We'll keep you overnight for observation. A precaution only," she added reassuringly.

Ivy nodded. They told her to lie still, then summoned the orderly to wheel her to a room in the obstetrics ward. By the time she was in a hospital gown and in bed in a semiprivate room—the other bed was empty—she was feeling much better. Drowsy, in fact.

She glanced at the steady drip of the IV and decided they'd probably given her a tranquilizer. But she didn't want to sleep. Quickly she pulled the telephone closer and dialed the hotel suite.

There was no answer, which she really hadn't expected, so she left a message for Max, telling him where she was.

After hanging up, she sighed heavily, as if she was very tired. Her eyes slid closed in spite of her efforts to remain alert.

Max dampened the fury that pounded through him as he entered Ivy's hospital room. She didn't need his anger, as Chuck had pointed out. Right now a sympathetic bedside manner was called for.

But he still wanted to pound the man who'd struck Ivy. His ire rose again at the thought that some slimeball would hit a woman, one holding a baby at that!

After speaking with the doctor, an older woman who had been confident neither Ivy nor the baby had suffered any serious damage, he'd headed straight for his fiancée's side.

Morgan Davis, who'd come to Ivy's rescue, said it had been a kidnapping attempt. The nerdy accountant, who had also helped, had thought so, too. So the danger wasn't to Ivy, per se, but to the baby being transferred to the adoption agency in the annex to the hospital.

How had the kidnappers known of the change of venue for the little girl?

They probably hadn't. Hospitals and adoption agencies were likely places to find babies, so they could have been checking out the area for days or weeks.

With a silent curse Max put the thoughts aside and

crossed the room. Ivy's eyes were closed and she lay utterly still. His heart gave a painful lurch.

Taking her hand, he thought she felt rather cool. He checked the monitor, which indicated her pulse and breathing were in the normal range. When the chemical cold pack slipped down to the pillow, it exposed a dark bruise along her jawline and running under her chin. She looked fragile and pale, as if she were an ethereal creature who might slip into a mist and disappear from this earth forever.

Don't get dramatic, he scolded his imagination. The woman doctor had said Ivy and the baby were fine, that the stay in the hospital was simply for observation.

Hooking a chair with his toe, he pulled it over and sat down without letting go of Ivy's hand. Never had he felt so fiercely protective of another.

And never so possessive. She was his, by heaven, and anyone who hurt her would pay a steep price if he had anything to say about it!

The afternoon crept by. He had several conferences with Chuck about security at the hospital, then more with Trent Crosby after Chuck called him with the news about his sister.

Trent and Katie came by at five. They held a whispered conference with Max, identical worried expressions on their faces as they tried to figure out this latest happening.

Ivy opened her eyes abruptly and glanced around.

"Easy," a soothing, familiar voice said.

She grasped Max's hand tightly, glancing from

him to her older siblings. "Trent, Katie, what are you doing here?" She frowned. "Where am I?"

"The hospital," Katie told her.

"Oh, the man…and the woman who wasn't old at all. They tried to take the baby."

"Which you held on to like a tigress," Trent said, giving her an approving grin. "Madison is safe in the adoption nursery."

"Did the police capture the couple?"

Max held the straw to her lips so she could drink when she reached for the water glass.

"No, but don't worry," he told her. "Morgan put a guard at the door of the nursery."

"Do you know Morgan?" Ivy asked in surprise.

His smile was sardonic but gentle. "I think I've met everyone who has any connection to you. They've called or stopped by in droves this afternoon. By the way, your friend Emma is down the hall."

"Em! How is she doing? I meant to come see her this afternoon." She realized being in the hospital herself was a good reason for forgetting her friend's surgery.

"She's fine. Morgan says he'll bring her over as soon as the surgeon gives the okay."

Ivy perused the empty bed in her room. "She could stay in here." A smile lit her face. "It would be just like old times when we were all home from college. Remember, Katie?"

Katie nodded.

"No way," Max declared. "You two would probably talk into the wee hours of the morning."

"They would," Trent told him. "It used to drive me crazy when the girls had their friends over for a slumber party. It was giggles and gossip all night long."

"You were so dense," Katie scoffed. "Our friends wanted to stay over so you would notice them. You never did, not even when they let you catch them in their sexiest pajamas when we raided the kitchen."

"I was an older man," Trent explained with a superior smile. "Teenagers were beneath my radar."

The four laughed and chatted for an hour, then the brother and sister departed. The nurse came in and took Ivy's temperature and blood pressure. In the hall, the rattle of the dinner trays was heard.

"I'm hungry," Ivy said. "I don't recall having lunch."

"Neither do I. Too much was happening today."

"There's a decent cafeteria here," the nurse told Max, giving him an approving smile. "Are you having any pain?" she asked Ivy.

"Some in the lower back again, but not as bad as when I was first brought in."

The nurse wrote on the chart, then made an adjustment in the IV flow rate. "That should make you comfortable."

"Thank you. Am I still having contractions?"

"Some, but nothing to worry about."

After the nurse left, Max pulled his chair close and took Ivy's hand again. His smile was sweet, slightly ironic, but amused. "So my queen is a fighter," he said softly. "I'll have to make sure the word gets out in Lantanya."

"Why?"

"I don't want any overeager citizen hurt by rushing up to you and getting bashed."

Ivy grimaced. "I did hit the man when he wouldn't let go. I guess that's why he socked me." She fingered her jaw, which was now pretty sore.

"You gave him some grief. Morgan said there was blood running from the guy's mouth. He must've bit his lip or tongue."

"That reminds me—his beard was false. It moved when I gave him the upper cut. The old woman wasn't old at all. She'd drawn wrinkles on her face with makeup. Her gray hair was probably a wig. She moved fast enough when she dashed for the car so they could get away."

"So Morgan said." He sighed in disgust. "That accountant chased the car, but didn't think to get the license number. Morgan stayed with you, so he didn't get it either, but he did recognize the make and model. The police are on the lookout for it."

"It was blue," Ivy said, recalling the fact.

Max nodded.

Her dinner tray was brought in at that moment. "Why don't you go down to the cafeteria and get something?" she suggested, worried that he was famished.

"Good idea. I'll bring it up and we can eat together." He paused at the door. "There's a guard in the hall. Chuck is talking to the police detectives and will report in later. Nothing like this will happen to you again."

Nodding, she watched him leave. He'd meant they would have a bodyguard for her, she mused as the meal was placed on a table and rolled into position beside her bed.

This was what her life would be like, married to Max. Hers and the baby's. Watched over constantly. Surrounded by guards. Always alert for dangers they couldn't see.

It was something to think about.

Chuck was on the phone when Max entered the suite later that evening. Max waved and headed for his and Ivy's bedroom. He stripped and went into the shower, his mood introspective as he bathed, the scent of her shampoo and powder and perfume filling the air.

Funny how quickly he thought of this space as hers as well as his. It was as if she'd always been a part of his life, as if she belonged there.

Fate? Predestination?

It didn't matter, not as long as the future belonged to both of them. And to their children.

Scenes of his childhood ran through his mind as he dried off, then dressed in fresh jeans and a shirt. With warm socks and comfortable sneakers, a clean handkerchief—his mother had never permitted him or his father to leave the family quarters without fresh hankies—and his wallet, he was ready. He left the bedroom.

"You heading back to the hospital?" Chuck asked, hanging up the hotel phone and his cell phone at the same time, looking pleased.

Max smiled. His security chief often carried on two or three conversations simultaneously. "Yes. Are you coming?"

"Not now. I'm waiting for a call. What time do you plan to be in tonight?"

"I'm not. I'll stay with Ivy."

Chuck gave him a thoughtful perusal, then nodded. "You can probably use the other bed. I've already told the hospital staff that no one but Ivy can be in the room due to security. Trent is sending his best men for twenty-four-hour duty. The sheriff has stationed a cruiser in the area, too. I've talked to the FBI and the State Department. They're leaving everything in our hands at the present. I, uh, explained about the family wedding and the formal one, so that's taken care of."

"Good."

When the cell phone rang, Chuck paused before picking up the call. "Have you told the rose how you feel about her?" he asked softly before snapping the phone open and answering.

Max frowned over the question as he drove Ivy's car to the hospital. Love. That was what Chuck was talking about.

Was it love to feel as if your heart had been ripped out of your body and put through a shredder the way his had when he'd learned Ivy had been hurt?

That was as close as he could come to describing the sensation.

The anger had followed upon learning the circumstances. Anger was good. It was clean and clear and direct with no muddy swirl of other emotions to confuse a person.

At the hospital, he parked and hurried to Ivy's room. The reassuring woman doctor was there, Dr. Glassis. So was Dr. Woodruff, who was Ivy's personal physician. Ivy was looking mulish.

"What's happening?" Max inquired, going to the far side of the bed and taking Ivy's hand, some part of him noting with pleasure that she returned his clasp.

"I've just told Ivy to stay off her feet for the next four or five days, other than meals and baths," the male doctor said firmly.

"I have things to do," she informed him.

"I agree with Dr. Woodruff," the older woman said, smiling at Ivy. "You need to stay off your feet. It's a simple precaution."

Ivy gave them a frown. "But you both said everything looks fine. If that's true, why can't I return to work?"

Max decided to put in his two cents' worth. "You've been through a trauma. Your body has taken a punch to the face and a kick to the abdomen. It's good sense to take it easy and let it recover completely. Or don't you care about the child?"

She bristled as he'd expected. "Of course I care about the baby! But sitting at a desk isn't physically taxing."

Max glanced at her, then the doctors. "How about if she rests tomorrow, then goes in for a half day on Monday?"

Dr. Woodruff consented with a nod. Dr. Glassis also concurred, smiled at all of them and announced she had to go.

"I will be your devoted slave," Max promised Ivy, "and will do all your errands."

"The wedding—" she began.

"Is in good hands," he told her.

"I see she's in good hands, too," Dr. Woodruff stated. The young doctor smiled and left them to argue it out.

"Good night. And thanks," Max called after him. He studied Ivy, a half smile lingering on his face. His rose had her thorns out.

"What?" she finally asked.

"I was thinking of our future," he murmured, leaning over to claim the kiss he hadn't gotten upon entering.

In spite of her anger, it only took a couple of seconds for her lips to go soft and responsive. He took his fill of the honey of her mouth, heat shooting off random sparks in his body as the hunger grew.

When he gazed down at her, she smiled tentatively, then sighed. "There's so much to do."

"Katie told me everything is planned and under control. She'll take care of any snags. I'll help. You can direct."

Her smile widened. "Mmm, that sounds like an offer I can't refuse."

"Con artist," he accused as he bent to her lips again.

"Ahem," said a voice behind them.

"Emma!" Ivy was obviously pleased to see her friend. "How are you feeling?"

"Fine," the other woman said as her husband pushed her into the room in a wheelchair. "This is just for fun. I don't really need it." She indicated the chair.

"I insisted," Morgan told them.

"Have you seen the news?" Emma asked. "You're a hero. So are Morgan and Everett. There's supposed to be the full story on the local station about now."

Ivy looked confused. "About the kidnapping attempt?"

Max smiled at her surprise and flicked on the TV so they could catch the news. A picture of Ivy standing beside a man Max didn't know came on the screen as the reporter told of Ivy's recent fund-raising for Children's Connection, then used that information as a lead-in to the kidnapping incident.

"Morgan Davis, the director of the adoption agency, joined in the struggle to prevent the kidnapping," the commentator explained.

There followed an interview with Morgan as he told of leaving his office to attend a luncheon meeting and seeing Ivy struggling with the two culprits.

"Everett Baker, an accountant for the agency, also aided in thwarting the attempt. Police are looking for a male and his female partner for questioning," the reporter said.

Several shots of the hospital and adoption agency annex were shown. Police were seen questioning

Morgan, Everett and the E.R. medic who had intervened on Ivy's and the baby's behalf.

The story ended with details of Morgan's work with a camp for older children who hadn't been adopted and Ivy's volunteer activities at Portland General and at Children's Connection.

"See?" Emma demanded. "You're both heroes."

"Ivy took the brunt of it," Morgan said, stepping forward to check out her bruised chin. He grinned and spoke to Max. "You should take a picture so your children can see her battle scars when you tell them the story."

Max laughed as Ivy protested showing off her injuries.

From the hall came the sound of a bell.

"Visiting hours are over," Emma told them. "I suppose we should get back to my room and let you rest."

"I'm not sleepy," Ivy declared. "Actually I'm hungry."

"You ate all your dinner," Max said.

Ivy nodded. "It was good. The hospital has a great chef directing the kitchen. But now I'm hungry for ice cream or a chocolate soda. A banana split would be nice."

Emma started laughing. "Food cravings. I always wanted things like hot peppers."

Max flashed Ivy an amused smile. "Okay, I'll go to the cafeteria and see what I can find."

"There's a frozen yogurt machine," Ivy told him, "and lots of toppings like fudge sauce and granola. And a cherry, if they have any."

"I'd like that, too," Emma said.

The men left the women and went in search of the treat. Upon returning, they pushed the other bed to the side and arranged chairs in a comfortable semi-circle around Ivy. The two couples ate and discussed the case, then segued to the wedding plans.

"Where will you go for a honeymoon?" Emma asked.

Ivy looked at Max. It was plain she hadn't thought that far ahead.

He gave her his most reassuring smile. "We will return to Lantanya so the people of my country can meet their queen."

"What does that mean?" Ivy asked worriedly.

"When our plane arrives, the citizens will line the streets for a glimpse of you. I thought we would use a touring car with a clear Plexiglas roof."

"Bulletproof?" Morgan asked, glancing from Max to Ivy and back.

"Yes." Max waited for Ivy's comment. He realized he was concerned about her answer, afraid that she might back out as she realized the demands and expectations to be made of her.

Her throat moved as she swallowed, then her smile appeared. "Does that mean I can make faces and stick my tongue out at them and they can't hit me with rocks?" she asked innocently.

A vast relief flooded his heart. "Absolutely."

"I won't do anything to embarrass you," she promised, becoming serious, "not even when I'm feeling grouchy and out of sorts."

Max realized he'd known that. "My mother practiced archery whenever she needed an outlet for frustration. She was a dead shot."

Ivy thought it over. "Tennis and jogging work for me. Is there a trail I can use?"

"Yes, all around the inside perimeter of the castle walls. There are turrets with guards there, too. It's all rather medieval."

The three Americans stared at Max.

He shrugged. "You get used to it." But he was aware of the flicker of unease across Ivy's lovely countenance.

Twelve

Ivy was released from the hospital on Sunday morning. That night, she slept in Max's arms, wonderfully secure and happy to be there. His good-night kisses were strictly platonic—very gentle, very caring, making her feel cherished and special to him.

She wondered if his care and gentleness would carry over into their marriage. After all, anyone could be nice for a couple of weeks, but marriage was for the long haul.

There can be no divorce, he'd told her.

It came to her just before she fell asleep that she'd accepted what fate seemed to have decreed for them. No matter how the marriage turned out, their union would be forever. That was the way she wanted it.

On Monday Max drove her to the office at Crosby

Systems to start clearing out her desk. Her second-in-command would take over her assigned duties, other than the Lantanya contract. She would continue as project manager for that.

A sense of satisfaction swept over her. She and Max had discussed her career. He had been the one to suggest that she continue with the educational system development. His approval of her continuing with the work had pleased her.

"How are you?" Trent asked, meeting her and Max in the hallway outside his office when they arrived.

"Sore but functional," she told her big brother.

Yesterday she'd talked to their younger brother, Danny, for more than an hour, filling him in on all that was happening and telling him of the wedding.

She'd wondered if he would come, but hadn't pressed him for an answer when she'd extended an invitation. Danny had his own problems.

By noon Max and Chuck had carted her personal items to her car and to Chuck's rental vehicle. Ivy gave her plants to the department secretary and a decorative vase she'd splurged on to Katie. She realized as she and Max left she had no need to return to the company founded by her father.

Pausing by the car, she looked back at the building and the wide lawn and lovely landscaping leading to the entrance. It felt odd to leave and know she wouldn't return.

"Feeling nostalgic already?" Max asked.

She managed a smile. "I've been free to come and

go here most of my life. At times Crosby Systems has felt more like home than anyplace I've ever lived. The lobby guard has been here over thirty years. I know him and his wife, his daughter, his grandchildren…."

A painful knot formed in her throat.

"You'll be leaving this far behind and going to a new place, one filled with strangers who will note your every word and action." It was as if he continued her thoughts. "It will be difficult, more so at first, but the spotlight will never completely go away. If we fight, if our children get into trouble, it will be fodder for the paparazzi."

Their eyes met over the roof of the car.

"But you will be there for me," she said softly.

His glance never wavered. "Always."

She settled in the familiar sedan. "What will I do with my car? And my furniture? Sell them," she answered before he could speak. "Trent and Katie will help."

"Your mother might do something," Max suggested, cranking the engine, then heading for the freeway.

Silence fell between them.

Max chuckled dryly. "I suppose not."

"We learned not to depend on her," Ivy murmured. "If I asked her to help with the wedding, she would take over, but it would become *her* day, not ours."

"Between Trent and Katie and you, all is taken care of, so there's no need to involve her."

"That's what I thought," Ivy agreed, relieved that

he understood so completely. She was lost in intro-
spection for a few minutes, then asked, "Max, is
there a book of protocol that I can read so I'll have
some idea of how to act in your country? Do I walk
a couple of steps behind you the way Prince Philip
does with Queen Elizabeth?"

"It's our country," he corrected. "And you'll walk
at my side as my queen."

Ivy had to smile. He hadn't a clue how arrogantly
sure of himself, and her, he had sounded. It came naturally to him, but she wasn't so sanguine.

"There are instructions," he said. "They've been
collected over the past five hundred years or so and
put into a leather-bound set. The minister of state has
assistants who can help if you have any questions on
the exact protocol."

Ivy gulped at the task ahead.

Max started laughing.

"You're teasing me," she accused, not sure
whether to be furious with him or grateful that he
wasn't concerned.

"Because you're so cute when you're mad," he
said, then laughed when she huffed in indignation.

To her surprise, he drove to the country club. "Are
we having lunch here?" she asked when he took her
arm and escorted her inside to a private room.

The place was decorated with pots of white and
golden mums with wide bands of white satin ribbons
around them. Smiling faces observed her and Max
with open interest from every table crowded into the
large banquet room. A long table next to the far wall

was laden with gaily wrapped packages that could only be bridal gifts.

Katie stood beside an empty chair at the head table. "Don't just stand there," she ordered. "We're ready to start the shower."

Ivy noticed her mother and stepmother were also present, but on opposite ends of the table.

"I'll see you later," Max murmured while all Ivy's friends applauded and called out greetings. "Chuck and I are having lunch in the dining room here with your father and Trent. Keep a stiff upper lip," he advised.

To her amazement, he lightly kissed her on the lips in front of everyone, then quickly left.

She placed a hand over her heart and gave her friends a mock frown. "I'm not sure I can take many more shocks this week," she told them.

At Katie's beckoning gesture, she took the seat of honor and proceeded with the luncheon, then opened packages that contained both wedding and baby gifts. Three hours passed in a blur of marriage advice, laughter, ribbons, lovely gift paper and oohs and aahs.

Max returned for her as soon as she finished the cake and coffee that ended the festivities. Katie and Toni shooed her away, assuring her they would take care of the gifts.

Sheila latched on to Max's arm and smiled prettily up at him. "I've been thinking," she told him. "Ivy will need someone close to help her when you two return to Lantanya. As her mother, I'm the logical choice—"

"We will be secluded on our honeymoon for the first weeks," Max interrupted with a kind smile. "Naturally we'll expect the family to attend the coronation and official wedding ceremonies. I hope you can reserve November for a visit with us."

He deftly hooked an arm around Ivy and led her from the room before Sheila could do more than murmur "Of course" and look chagrined at being thwarted in her plans.

Behind her, Ivy heard Katie call to their mother and ask her help in packing up the gifts.

"You do that so well," Ivy murmured to Max when he held her arm as she climbed into the car.

"Practice," he said after tipping the valet and leaving the parking area. "Do you think the United States is the only place with persons who need to be put in their place?"

"I've never thought about it," she admitted. "I had better observe and learn from you, I suppose."

He braked at a stop sign and glanced at her. "I'll be considerate of your mother, my love, but I won't allow her or anyone to intrude into our private time. After the wedding on Sunday, I intend to have you to myself as much as possible." He touched her cheek. "I need that." He paused. "I need you," he said softly.

An odd sensation attacked Ivy's insides. It was as if something deep in the most secret place of her soul had been opened up and exposed to the light for the first time. She felt vulnerable but oddly happy.

"It's nice to be needed," she told him.

What about loved? some sly part of her inquired.

She was lost in thought the rest of the way to the hotel. In the suite, Max insisted she rest on the sofa when she refused to go to bed, while he and his security advisor spoke with the courier who'd been waiting for them to return. Chuck unlocked the handcuffs that secured the diplomatic bag to the man's wrist.

Closing her eyes, Ivy contemplated the changes one romantic, impulsive night could have on a person for all time. Would her one night be worth all the nights that would follow when she joined Max in a new life in a new place? Would there be loneliness? Regret?

She had to live through it to know.

Saturday morning dawned, but not brightly. A rosy mist surrounded the sunrise before the sun disappeared under a heavy layer of clouds driven in from the Pacific by a cold wind. Rain was predicted that afternoon and into the night.

Ivy, still in bed, sipped coffee and observed the swirl of a low ground fog while Max talked on the phone.

"Yeah. Ahh," he said in understanding. "Good work, ol' man." He laughed at something the other party said. "Good. That's great. Yes. Don't worry, I trust you and Mrs. Bartlett completely. Everything sounds perfect."

Ivy glanced at him when he replaced the phone.

"That was Ned Bartlett, the valet I told you about."

"I remember," she said. "Uh, am I allowed to ask

you any questions about conversations I overhear, such as now? Or is that against the rules?"

He rose and stretched leisurely. Ivy admired his masculine grace and the ripple of muscles in his naked chest and arms. Pajama bottoms covered the rest of his body. He'd been sleeping in them that week, giving her a chaste kiss each night and settling beside her in sleep. She'd missed their lovemaking.

A low chuckle drew her attention back to his face. Realizing she'd been staring at his torso, she smiled and murmured, "Caught me."

He settled on the side of the bed and leaned close to claim her mouth in a heart-jarring kiss. "I like it when you look at me," he admitted, "especially when you're lusting after my body."

"I am not!" She had to compress her lips to keep from laughing after her indignant denial.

"Yes, you are. And yes, it's okay for you to ask me anything you like. With your active intelligence, you would go crazy if I tried to keep secrets. I won't do that to you. You'll be my mate in every way, sharing the good and the bad of running a small kingdom to the best of our ability."

She caressed his chest, loving the warmth of his skin, the crisp sensation of the dark hairs under her fingers, the knowledge that she was free to touch him like this in their private moments.

"I've missed you—" She stopped abruptly, realizing she was giving away more of her inner thoughts than she wanted to admit, arrogant male that he was.

He pressed her hands to his chest. "I've missed

our lovemaking, too, but I wanted to let you rest and recover completely from the trauma you suffered last week. Tomorrow will be the wedding, and then…" He leaned close. "Then you will be mine forever. I intend to make love to you every night for years and years."

A thrill of anticipation shot through her.

"We will have a good marriage," he whispered as he kissed her cheek near her ear. "Stay in bed as long as you want. We have the rehearsal dinner tonight, so it will be late before we get in, I suspect."

She nodded, knowing he'd arranged the meal at the country club, which would take place after the rehearsal at her father and stepmother's home. When he headed for the bathroom, she propped the pillows a bit higher behind her, refilled her coffee cup and picked up the first section of the newspaper.

Hearing the shower come on, she considered joining him and seeing if she could tempt him into indulging their passion now. No, she decided. That wouldn't be right. Max had shown exemplary control all week. She would do the same.

And he was right. After tomorrow night, they would have the rest of their lives together and could make love every night. The thought brought such a rush of blood and whirling emotions to her head that she became dizzy.

Bringing herself firmly under control, she read of the troubles of the world, the global economy and a new outbreak of SARS cases in Hong Kong and China.

After Max had bathed, dressed and joined Chuck in the living room, Ivy rose and prepared for the day, too.

Forty minutes later, standing at the window and listening to Max and Chuck speak by phone to one of the ministers in Lantanya, she wondered if it was raining there, too. Here in Portland, the early-morning mist had turned into a steady rain that didn't bode well for the outdoor wedding she and Katie had planned so carefully.

She sighed. Well, best-laid plans and all that, as Robbie Burns had mentioned in a long-ago poem.

Hands touched her shoulders. "Are you worried about the wedding?" Max asked.

Glancing at him over her shoulder, she nodded. "I was wondering if we should change the ceremony to the church. But it may be too late for that," she added doubtfully.

"I have ordered sunshine for tomorrow," he told her, nuzzling her neck. "All will be well."

"Even so, the ground will be wet."

"Then we will put up a pavilion. Chuck has already checked with a company who rents equipment for weddings."

Ivy's eyes opened wide. "I am constantly amazed at the efficiency of those around you."

"They are paid to think of all contingencies."

The phone rang again. Chuck gestured for Max to pick up the other receiver in the suite after he answered.

Ivy listened to the one-sided conversation with the

minister of state of Lantanya. There was a question about the estates of the traitors who'd tried to take over the kingdom. If they confiscated the estates, should they exile the remaining family of the coup members?

"No," Max said after a brief conversation with Chuck. "I won't punish the families for the fathers' mistakes."

He glanced her way after he spoke, and she knew he was thinking of their child, heir to his kingdom.

A shiver trickled down her back in slow waves like a Chinese torture machine. All the uncertainties she'd experienced since confirming the pregnancy came back to haunt her.

Who was she, Ivy Crosby of Portland, Oregon, to marry into royalty and produce the future kings and queens who would decide the fate of a nation, small as it might be?

The questions remained even as Ivy dressed for the rehearsal dinner that night. Max hooked the back of her dress, then smiled at her through their reflections in the mirror. She returned the smile, pride stiffening her courage as she noted his commanding good looks in a dark suit and her own vivid coloring.

Her cheeks were flushed of their own accord, not from rouge, and her eyes sparkled, enhanced by the matching blue of her long evening dress, a new one with scalloped lace along the neckline, sleeves and hem.

"You look lovely," he said, admiration in his eyes.

"And you're as handsome as a prince," she teased, deciding a light tone was best. "By the way, who will help me with my hooks and zippers after we return to Lantanya?"

"The wife of my valet has let it be known that she expects to fill the position." Max caressed her cheek. "She'll adore you. And spoil the children."

"And I will let her." Ivy wrinkled her nose at him when he gave her a mock frown.

"I intend to do some spoiling of my own." He withdrew a velvet jewelry box from the bedside drawer. "The courier brought this from the palace vault."

Ivy could only stare as he touched a hidden spring and the box opened. Inside on black velvet was displayed the most magnificent necklace set of blue sapphires, surrounded by pure white diamonds, that she'd ever seen.

"Your engagement ring," Max said, slipping it on her finger. "The other ring you'll get tomorrow."

He indicated the wedding band, which was covered by alternating sapphires and diamonds. Lifting the necklace, he held it up to the light as they admired its sparkle, then he fastened it around her neck.

"Shall I do the earrings?" he asked.

She nodded. He carefully inserted the posts into her earlobes and slipped the security clasps into place.

"No tiara?" she asked, teasing, but her voice trembled in spite of her attempt to keep things light.

"Not with these," he said solemnly, "but there will be. Several, in fact, for different occasions."

"Oh, Max," she murmured in distress.

"You will be marvelous, my love." He dropped a kiss on the side of her neck. "Marvelous," he repeated huskily.

Her fingers trembled uncontrollably as she touched the cool stones in the necklace. "Princess Di had sapphires, too," she said, but only to herself when Max answered a summons at the bedroom door.

"The car is here," Chuck told them.

"Ready?" Max asked, taking a stole from Chuck. He draped the blue-tinged white fox fur around her shoulders.

"I've never worn fur," Ivy said.

"Fur and leather work are our major industries on Lantanya. However you feel privately, you must never disparage it or refuse to accept a gift from the guild that produces items such as this."

She nodded in understanding, but all the time she was wondering what she was doing. As soon as they arrived at her father's house for the rehearsal, Katie pulled her into the bedroom where they left their jackets and purses.

"You're flushed," her sister said, touching the back of her hand to Ivy's forehead. "Are you okay?"

"I don't know," Ivy said. "Katie—" She didn't know what else to say.

"Oh, God," Katie said fatalistically. "You aren't backing out, are you?"

A pain shot straight to Ivy's heart at the idea. "No," she said, then stronger, "no, I couldn't. I couldn't do that to Max."

Because I love him too much, was the rest of that statement, left unsaid. Her knees went rubbery at the thought.

"Good. Besides, you've already given up your apartment and had the furniture put in storage." Katie patted her cheek. "Max is a good person, little sis. I knew it the first time I met him."

That drew a smile from Ivy. "I trust your judgment, O great wise one."

Katie rolled her eyes. "I know I got you that blind date with the jerk from college, but anybody can make one mistake."

"This mistake involves marriage." Ivy fingered the jewels around her neck.

Katie did a double take. "Ivy, they're the most beautiful things I've ever seen! Max gave them to you? Of course he did," she answered herself. "When?"

"Just before we left the hotel."

"Wow," Katie murmured as they left the room and went to join the rest of the wedding party. "Hey, you can give me your cast-off evening dresses the way Princess Diana did with her friends. We'll be so glamorous our friends won't recognize us anymore."

Her sister pushed her glasses up on her nose and laughed at the idea. Ivy smiled, then considered Katie's practical two-piece evening pantsuit. It was a simple black outfit, smart and dressy but very plain. It was a bit loose and didn't do a thing for Katie's new slimmer figure.

Maybe, Ivy thought, it was time for her and

Katie to learn to be more fashionable and less...
business oriented. Neither of them had ever learned
to flirt—

"Ah, the minister is here," Katie said, breaking
into the rather odd musing. "We're ready," she called
out, guiding Ivy into the living room.

The rehearsal took place in the library. Chuck was
Max's best man, and Trent was the groomsman. Danny
would have been the other, but he didn't appear. Ivy
hadn't expected him to come, but she still missed him.

Katie and Emma walked side by side as her maid
and matron of honor, then she and her father practiced walking down an imaginary aisle. Her eyes
met Max's when the brief practice session was over.
He gave her a slight wink, his eyes alight with mis-
chief. As if he'd spoken in her mind, she knew he was
thinking of having his wicked way with her.

She looked down before her thoughts could give
her away. He chuckled and took her arm. "Let's go.
I'm starved," he told her.

At the country club, a private room was ready for
them, again with white and golden mums adding a
festive air to the surroundings. An arch made of bal-
loons with Congratulations spelled out in glittering
golden letters welcomed the bridal pair. The manager greeted them and presented a bottle of expensive
champagne to them, then discreetly retreated.

For Ivy, the evening felt more and more surreal as
it wore on, as if none of this were happening. Max's
touch on her wrist reminded her that it was. Very definitely.

* * *

Trent took an opportunity while the women were repairing their makeup and the men were enjoying cigars after dinner to discuss with Max and Chuck as well as his father the latest findings on security.

"You were right," he said to Chuck. "The bugging of Ivy's phone was an inside job. As you suggested, we gave the culprit enough rope and he did, indeed, hang himself."

Chuck nodded in satisfaction. "You got him."

"We did. It was a programmer we hired last year to work on the Lantanya project. He came to us from a Silicon Valley company and had a great recommendation from his former boss. No wonder. He was feeding info back to them on the setup of the educational system, both hardware and software."

"The traitor," his father muttered.

"Right," Trent agreed. "They wanted the new router design, but Ivy kept the drawings under lock and key and only gave out parts of the design on a need-to-know basis. The guy wasn't in the loop, and thanks to Ivy's care, he couldn't find out what he needed to know."

"So what did he hope to gain by bugging her phones?" Max asked.

"Clues to where the system was being tested, if she had the drawings at home, anything they could get a hold of," Trent explained.

"How did you catch him?" Jack Crosby asked.

"Chuck told us to hire a new computer guru who was supposedly an expert on running the tests that integrated the hardware with the software. Naturally our expert was really an expert at company espionage. When one of the programmers expressed an interest in the tests and made a practice of hanging around and got real chummy, our man let him, feeding him just enough to indicate the expert knew the whole system and had the entire design set."

"Ah," his father said with a pleased expression as he puffed on the cigar.

"This afternoon our man caught the other guy going through his office files, which he'd conveniently left unlocked, and copying those marked with the Lantanya project code name," Trent finished, leaning back in the chair with a pleased grin.

"Trent called me shortly before we left the hotel," Chuck said, taking up the tale. "The D.A. has a warrant and is now searching the man's apartment as we speak. The cops have already traced the culprit's e-mails to their source, so we know who was on the receiving end of his messages and directing him in the espionage."

"Good work," Max told Trent and Chuck. "I'm pleased with the business contract we have with Crosby Systems and the level of cooperation you've given Chuck in this."

Jack Crosby chuckled. "It could prove a bit awkward if we didn't cooperate. After all, as my son-in-law, you'll have an inside source within the company."

"Your daughter, sir, can be very closemouthed when she wishes," Max murmured, bringing laughter to the men, which included Morgan Davis, but not the minister, who'd had to leave when the meal was over.

"It has been a pleasant experience for me that all my children are involved in the company," Jack continued, his manner introspective. He gave Trent a mock frown. "I hope you will take a hint from your sister and produce an heir. We need children. I didn't realize how much while my own were growing up. Young people add energy to life. They're our hope for the future."

Max recognized regret in the older man's eyes as he paused, then smiled, as if in apology for his serious tone.

Jack's eyes went to the door. "Here are the women."

Max's gaze was drawn from his future father-in-law to the end of the room. Sheila Crosby entered first, her manner disclosing a mixture of pride and determined confidence. Her ex-husband's second wife was behind her, looking as lovely as a high-fashion model.

Emma, Katie and Ivy came in as a group, all smiling. Ivy was slender and erect, as regal as a queen. *His* queen.

Max tensed as an odd feeling flashed over him. His heart gave a sort of lurch, then a painful contraction as he stood and waited for his bride to join them. He didn't understand the feeling at all.

"Have you men solved the problems of the world?" Emma demanded as they prepared to leave.

"Just this corner of it," Jack assured her. He clasped his daughters about the shoulders. "With beauties such as these around us, the problems seem small."

Both Katie and Ivy looked surprised by this, but Max understood their father's sentiment. There was something about a woman's loveliness and gentle bearing, about marriage and family and the trust implied by those, that made a man proud.

Thirteen

"You're restless," Chuck said, studying his friend the next afternoon at the hotel.

Max grimaced. "Why does time pass so slowly when you want it to rush, and yet go so fast when you want it to slow down?"

"Now let me see…how am I to interpret that?" Chuck murmured aloud as if discussing Max's question with a third party. "Does he want time to pass fast or to slow down? Is this wedding jitters or eagerness?"

Turning from the window, Max smiled at his best bud. "I'm ready," he said.

"Ah, the rose has truly captured the elusive playboy prince, has she?"

Max ignored that. "It's time you were thinking of

hearth and home and all that, too. You're not getting any younger, old man."

"Yeah, well, I had a good time before I lost my hair and my teeth." He rose from the sofa and joined Max at the window. The afternoon shadows were growing longer. "It's time we left."

"Good. This place is too quiet, like a morgue."

"You miss her," Chuck murmured.

Ivy had left early that morning for her father's house, driving herself now that the culprit behind the break-in and bugging of her place had been arrested. She didn't know that she'd been followed by four security men, in a motorcycle, a delivery van, an SUV and a family sedan.

Max paused at the door of the hotel suite. "It's an odd feeling. I worry about her when she isn't in my sight. I was raised to be responsible for a kingdom, but I've never thought about those feelings transferring to a person."

The two men walked down the corridor to the elevator. "I suppose it's natural," Chuck said. "Ivy has been in the thick of company espionage and that rather inept kidnapping attempt. However, I don't think any of it was directed at her personally."

"You think no one has it in for her, then?" Max asked sardonically.

"No more than for you. Shall I drive?"

Max nodded and got in the passenger side of the car, which was waiting at the door. "Thanks for your help on everything. As usual, you came through like a champ."

"We aim to please," Chuck said modestly, but spoiled it with a know-it-all grin.

Max relaxed each set of muscles as he'd learned to do from his father. It dispelled tension and allowed one to think more clearly. However, there was a tightness in his chest that he couldn't ease. It was annoying.

"The day couldn't be better," Chuck said when they turned into the drive of the Crosby estate where a guard checked their credentials before allowing them to proceed. "Yesterday's rain cleared the air. The sun dried everything up today. The weather is perfect for a wedding."

"Yeah, Ivy was worried about that." Max gave a half smile. "I told her I'd ordered sunshine for today. I'm glad Mother Nature didn't show us who's boss."

At the handsome mansion, the two men surveyed the preparations for the wedding. Three florist vans were pulled discreetly to the side of the house. A raised walkway, covered in red carpet, led to a pavilion covered by a white tent. The filmy white walls of the tent were artfully draped and tied at the corners, opening it to the lovely vista on all sides.

One end of the main tent opened on a gazebo, also white and covered with silk braided with wide, colored ribbons at each corner. Pennants of blue, gold and black, the colors of the Lantanya flag, wafted in the gentle breeze like medieval banners.

Magnificent sprays of fall flowers in white baskets lined the aisle leading to the gazebo where the vows would be exchanged. The two steps and the floor of the outdoor structure were covered in the red carpet with a white satin runner ending at an altar woven of pink, white and golden roses on a trellis. Candelabras flanked the altar.

The minister would stand in front of it while the couple stood on the first step. There they would exchange vows of trust and fidelity until death.

"Did you bring the rings?" Max asked.

Chuck removed the gold bands from his pocket to show that he had them. The groom's ring had no jewels, as Ivy's did, but it was engraved with their names and the date as was the bride's wedding band.

"I'll give your ring to Katie as soon as I see her," the best man promised.

"Good." Max checked his watch. "Almost time. I suppose we should report in."

"We've been spotted. I saw Katie at a window when we first arrived. Look, the driveway and parking area are almost full. I thought this was to be a small affair."

"Ivy has lived here all her life," Max said as they headed for the side door to the house. "I'm sure she has many friends she couldn't leave out."

Trent greeted them when they entered the house, then led the way to a small parlor adjoining the library. The minister was there, looking dignified in a black robe.

From the front of the house came the sounds of many voices raised in greetings and several bursts of laughter.

"It's time," Trent said.

At that moment, soft music mysteriously began, a fairy melody heard from far away, beguiling the listener to follow its charming notes. Strangely, the crowd did just that. As if on cue, they left the house and gathered in the tent.

"Okay, this is it," the capable CEO announced. "I don't know why I'm nervous. I'm not the one tying the knot again."

Max knew that Trent had been married but was now divorced. He didn't want to think of the other man's unkind fate in picking the wrong woman. Not that he was worried about that being the case with him.

Ivy was everything he wanted in a wife. The marriage was a wise arrangement, with mutual respect and a strong physical attraction on both sides.

I love you, love you, love you.

She'd said that in passion. But not since then. The tightness in his chest increased. He frowned, not sure what it meant. The solemnity of marriage he recognized. He felt that. But other emotions jostled inside him, confusing him with an urgency to do something.

He unclenched his hands and took a calming breath as Trent peered out the window.

"You are nervous," Chuck murmured.

"Not about the wedding."

"The wedding-night retreat is ready. I checked it out myself this morning. It's secluded enough to suit your tastes."

"Thanks."

Trent gestured to them and the minister. "There's the signal. You first, sir," Trent said to the preacher. He held the door for the other three men to precede him.

The unsettling sensation expanded in Max's chest as he stood at the gazebo and waited for Ivy and her attendants. Annoyed, he suppressed the unidentified emotions and turned to the crowd.

The music changed. Max spotted the organist on the patio behind the house. From her vantage point, she could observe the pavilion and the ceremony. Sheila and Toni were seated in the front row on the bride's side. For a second he felt the loss of his own parents, then he cleared his mind and concentrated on the present.

Katie and Emma, looking very pretty and properly serious, appeared and came down the aisle together. When "The Wedding March" began, everyone stood.

Ivy and her father, with stately movements, swept toward the gazebo. She was the perfect vision in white, the most beautiful creature he had ever seen.

Max's heart gave a giant contraction, so swift and painful he was almost staggered by the force of it.

Let her be happy. Let me be worthy.

The prayer stole into his consciousness. For the first time since the engagement, he worried that he might fail…that she might hate her new home…the constrictions of palace life…him…

Her eyes met his. She smiled, and it was like sun-

shine melting the ice that had invaded his heart.
Logic prevailed. Ivy would never forsake her vows.
She would stay for duty's sake, if nothing else. And
for their child.

"Dearly beloved," the minister began.

The ceremony was traditional and soon done.
Photographs were taken quickly, then they were off
to the reception at the country club. A much larger
crowd awaited them there.

For nearly an hour he and Ivy stood in the receiving line and greeted their guests. His bride was as
gracious as any queen, her smiles generous, her gaze,
when she glanced at him, a bit questioning.

He realized he had hardly taken his eyes from her
since she'd walked down the aisle and pledged her
life to his.

"You are incredibly lovely," he murmured, bringing her hand to his lips. "I am overcome."

He'd meant to reassure her, but the words were
not mere gallantry. He was entranced by her, his
princess of the roses. The tightness invaded his chest
again.

The sweet shyness of their first encounter suffused her manner with just the right amount of in-
triguing reserve. He wanted the festivities to be over.
He needed to be alone with his rose.

Ivy was aware of something different about Max,
some subtle disquiet inside him that impinged on his
usual confident manner. Was he not happy about the
marriage? Or was he simply impatient to get the or-

deal over and return to his country where a thousand details of running a kingdom surely awaited him?

Uncertain about his thoughts, she felt chilled as they ate, endured endless toasts, then danced for hours.

"We should go," Max said shortly before midnight.

She nodded. After kissing her father, mother and stepmother, she turned to Trent and Katie. She hugged each of them closely as emotion filled her. "Thank you. Thank you both for being wonderful," she whispered.

"Be happy," Katie ordered, a break in her voice.

"We'll see you in November," Trent reminded her, his tone husky.

"And when the baby is born," Katie added.

Ivy tossed the bouquet, and Max did the garter bit, looking a bit sardonic at the ritual, then they were free to leave. She had no idea where they were going.

A car was waiting for them, a long, black limo, the driver smartly dressed in a black uniform, an assistant at his side. "A guard?" she asked.

Max nodded. "There will be others where we are going, but if all goes well, we won't see them."

"Where are we going? I assumed we would stay at the hotel. No?" she questioned when he smiled mysteriously.

"It's a secret place for only the two of us."

She liked the idea of a honeymoon cabin deep in the woods or high on a hill overlooking a lake or the river, somewhere as romantic as the resort in Lantanya had been.

It came to her that she wanted to recapture that night. She wanted to hear him call her "my love" again.

A silent sigh escaped her as their driver took them farther into the mountains east of the city. She must be practical about the marriage. During the past week, she'd accepted the fact that they could have a good union without sharing a wildly romantic love. As Max had said, they had mutual respect and passion. That was enough.

A ping of sadness echoed through her. Pushing it aside, she turned to him. "Are we almost there?" she asked in the plaintive manner of a child, her smile teasing.

"Almost," he murmured in a deep tone that started a vibration deep inside her.

I love this man, whatever he is, prince, king, husband, friend. I love him.

After climbing a steep, paved road, they stopped beside a large house built of logs, lights glowing from within.

"A lodge," she said. "How romantic."

He didn't utter a word, but simply took her hand and, helping her with her skirt, guided her from the vehicle and onto the broad front porch. The mountain air was cold, she noted, as if she were a spectator on the scene.

After opening the door, he swung her into his arms and stepped across the threshold, closing the door behind them. Setting her on the shining wooden floor, he locked the bolt, his gaze on her, that unsettling intensity in those fathomless depths once again.

Turning away, she glanced around. The beautiful golden mums that she liked decorated the room. A table was laid for two in front of a fire crackling in the grate.

"I thought we might be hungry," he said.

She nodded as words deserted her.

"Shall we change?" he asked. "Our luggage should be here."

"Oh, yes, that's a good idea."

He led the way to a master suite on one side of the huge cabin. Pink and white roses were everywhere.

"Max," she said in wonder, "this is so lovely."

"The roses are from home. From Lantanya. I had them flown here for us, for tonight."

It was such a thoughtful gesture, and so unexpectedly romantic, her chest filled with emotion. "Like that first night," she finally managed to say.

"Yes." He moved behind her. "Shall I help you with your dress? Is there a zipper?"

"At the side," she instructed, holding an arm up. "And a placket of buttons in front."

"Ah," he murmured in satisfaction.

Deftly, he unfastened the side opening, then, still behind her, he started on the tiny, silk-covered buttons that began at her throat and dipped to the center between her breasts. By the time he finished, her nipples were beaded in wanton anticipation of his caresses.

"I want you," she said, turning her head to look at him over her shoulder.

He slipped the wedding gown off her arms, then leaned down to kiss her shoulder and neck. She laid her head against him, swamped by tactile sensations.

When she was unable to stand it another second, she turned and snuggled into his arms, love and longing all mixed up inside her, demanding release.

"I've never felt this way," she admitted.

He cupped her face between his large but gentle hands. "How? Tell me how you feel."

She hesitated to confess her unrequited love, afraid he didn't want that much from her, that he would be content with the passion they shared.

"Tell me, my sweet rose," he whispered against her lips. "Tell me what I need to hear."

The deep sincerity of his tone, the vivid hunger in his gaze confused her. "Max? Is something wrong?"

His heavy exhalation touched her lips. "Now that it is a fait accompli, I wonder if you will regret the marriage." His smile was self-mocking. "I wonder if you will grow to hate it…and me."

Her heart contracted, then expanded to fill her whole body. "I could never hate you," she told him softly.

"Then tell me, before I kiss you, how you feel," he demanded.

He realized he needed to hear her words of love without the heady swirl of passion riding their senses. He needed to know why she'd stopped protesting the marriage and had accepted him as her mate. For a second, as she hesitated, he was aware of a pit of darkness before him, an abyss of unrelenting misery if she didn't care....

"I love you," she said. "I have from the moment you set the match to the cherries jubilee. It was like a spark igniting my heart, lighting a path to my very soul."

Relief speared through him as she smiled, her innate shyness flickering through her eyes. The strange tightness in his chest suddenly eased, too. He knew what it was now, recognized it and welcomed it even though it left him feeling open and vulnerable.

"You will be queen of my kingdom, but you'll always be the princess of my heart," he told her. "My sweetheart rose...my love..." He kissed her tenderly.

Ivy closed her eyes until she could control the happiness that flooded her with joy. Wrapping her arms around his strong shoulders, she gave herself to him, to the passion, as she had that magical night.

My love, he'd called her then. *My love,* he called her now.

With exquisite caresses, with sweet murmurings and laughter, he peeled away the layers of clothing, exposing more than their eager bodies and driving hunger for each other. They came together in mutual desire...and love.

"Max, I love you," she whispered on a sob as he made her vulnerable with his touch and his kisses, his wonderful, wonderful kisses....

Minutes or hours later they rested, then languidly rose. He placed a lush velour robe around her and slippers on her feet, then quickly donned sweats and thick socks.

"Ready to eat?" he asked, leading the way to the living room and the table laid before the fire.

She nodded, actually hungry for food now that other needs had been fulfilled. A blush warmed her face at his smile.

"So am I," he said.

There were various meats and accompaniments in the refrigerator. They filled their plates. When they were seated on each side of the small table, he raised a glass of champagne. "A toast."

She lifted her glass and waited.

"I've felt odd the past couple of days," he told her. "There was a tightness inside that I couldn't explain. Today I realized what it was."

His eyes told her before he said the words.

"I love you. I always will. You're the one I've been waiting for all my life. I had thought I was foolish to expect a great love, but fate or my guardian angel knew what I needed. You."

His gaze never wavering, he drank to her and them and their future together. She did, too. He spoke again.

"Be still, my heart, 'tis naught
But love that has wrought
This miracle of passionate delight,
And bliss of a most enduring sort."

She recalled the poem of the lovesick Lantanyan whom Max had quoted what seemed ages ago. Now she smiled as these new words settled softly in her heart like rose petals, to be preserved forever.

"My knight of the roses," she said, lifting her glass. "Champion of my heart and guardian of its treasures. May our love bloom eternal, a garden forever in the springtime of its flowering."

They drank of the heady nectar of shared love and pledged their troth to each other for all time. Then they sealed it with a kiss.

* * * * *

*Turn the page for a sneak preview of the next
emotional* LOGAN'S LEGACY *title,
FOR LOVE AND FAMILY
by bestselling author Victoria Pade
on sale in September 2004...*

"Come in," Terese Warwick called in answer to the knock on the hospital room door at nine o'clock that night.

After having given two pints of blood, staying long enough for the doctors in charge of the emergency room to see for themselves that her blood sugar level was back to normal and that she was able to stand without fainting or getting dizzy, she'd finally received the go-ahead to be released. So she was sitting in a chair in one corner, expecting her visitor to be a nurse with forms for her to sign.

But it wasn't a nurse whose head poked through the door. It was Hunter Coltrane.

"Are you decent?" he asked in the deepest, richest male voice she thought she'd ever heard.

"I never had to do anything but roll up my sleeve," she informed him with a laugh at that question. A laugh that was almost giddy for no reason at all, except maybe that she'd spent the entire time since she'd met the man thinking about him. Wondering about him.

"Come in," she said, trying not to sound as eager as she felt. And telling herself that she wasn't necessarily eager to see Hunter Coltrane in particular, that it was just that after so many hours in that room she was eager to see anyone.

Hunter Coltrane accepted the invitation, stepping inside and letting the door close behind him.

The room was small but there had been doctors and nurses in and out of it and none of them had seemed to fill the space the way this man did. He was a commanding presence—over six feet tall; with broad, muscular shoulders; long, thick-thighed legs; and a narrow waist and hips in between.

"How are you doing?" he asked.

"I'm fine. I felt a little weak and light-headed for a while, but they gave me juice and cookies and I'm okay now. They're letting me go home."

"The nurse told me before that you were getting out—that's why I'm here."

That sounded like it might evolve into a fast good-bye and Terese didn't want it to. Not before she knew how her nephew was. So she said, "More importantly, how is Johnny?"

If Hunter Coltrane had been about to make a quick exit it didn't show because he swung a leg over the wheeled stool the doctor had used and sat down across from her. "Johnny's okay," he announced with relief in his voice. "The nosebleed stopped. Finally. And the transfusion made him feel better. They're keeping him for forty-eight hours—something about checking his hemoglobin to make sure it stabilizes. But as long as he isn't bleeding, we're doing well."

"And during the forty-eight hours will they know if he has hemophilia or not?" The drive to the hospital had only taken about twenty minutes but Hunter Coltrane had filled her in on a few things along the way.

"Yeah, those results should be in before they let him go. They're pretty sure that's what we're dealing with, but they said it calls for caution and being aware of some things, but there's no reason to panic. It isn't a progressive kind of disease or something that he'll be sick or debilitated over. Which is good."

"In other words, it's not something you'd *want* him to have, but it could be worse," Terese summarized.

"Right. I'm sorry you couldn't come in and see him this whole time, though. The nurses told me you wanted to, but between the nosebleed and the transfusion, the poor kid was overwhelmed and not up for company."

"That's okay. I understand." But that didn't mean she hadn't been disappointed. She'd been hoping this would be an opportunity to meet her nephew. The nephew she probably wouldn't have any other chance to meet even though it was something she'd always wanted.

"Once the bleeding stopped," Hunter Coltrane was saying, "and the transfusion was over, Johnny was exhausted. He fell right to sleep."

Terese nodded. "I'm just glad he's okay."

"I'll be staying here with him, but since he's out like a light now I thought I could run you home without him missing me. I don't want you to have to take a cab home or bother anyone to pick you up."

"It's okay. I called the house when they told me I'd be able to leave and had a car sent to get me. But thanks for thinking of me."

The rancher's expression had relaxed once more and he laughed a wry laugh. "It's me who needs to be thanking you. I can't tell you how grateful I am that you came here and did this. I'm in your debt. If there's anything I can ever do to repay you…"

Terese didn't respond immediately to that. Slowly she said, "There is one thing I'd like."

"Anything," he said.

"Here's the thing, for the three days after Johnny was born—and before you took custody—my sister didn't want anything to do with him. But I hated the thought that he was only being looked after by nurses so I spent a lot of time there with him. I fed him and changed him and…" And she was getting teary-eyed just remembering it. Remembering how much it had broken her heart when she'd had to accept that her sister really wasn't going to keep him….

"Anyway," she said, "I fell in love with him and then he was gone and… Well, I've always wished I'd been able to keep in touch with him. To know him and how he's doing. To watch him grow up—even from a distance…"

Now it was Hunter Coltrane who didn't respond readily. Instead he seemed to be thinking it over. Or maybe he was just trying to come up with an excuse.

"Okay," the rancher said then, holding up one hand—palm outward—to stop more of the verbal avalanche she was in the midst of.

"Really?" she said.

"Really. And, you know, I have a guest cabin at the ranch. Nothing fancy, but if you wanted to come out and spend a few days with us, you could meet Johnny and get to know him a little on his own territory. What would you say to that?"

It was more than Terese had ever hoped for.

"That would be wonderful," she finally said.

"Great."

Another nurse knocked and opened the door just then, coming in with papers in hand for Terese to sign.

Hunter stood to give the stool over to her. "I'll get out of the way so you can go home. But I'll call you as soon as I get Johnny out of here and we can set up a time for you to come to the ranch."

"I can't wait," Terese answered as he left the room.

But as she smoothed her hair into place something else flashed through her mind—the image of Hunter Coltrane. The image of Hunter Coltrane with her…

"Now *that's* a pipe dream," she muttered to herself.

And no one knew it better than Terese.

Because Hunter Coltrane was handsome enough to stop traffic and that reflection of herself left her without any doubts that she was hardly the kind of woman who would so much as turn his head.

Plain—that's what she was.

She left the hospital room, telling herself to just be glad she was going to get to meet her nephew.

And working to erase the lingering mental image of her nephew's father.

The mental image that had things inside her sitting up and taking notice.

Just the way the man himself had....